FIRE CANOE FINNEGAN

Denis J. Harrington
and
Charlie Steel

FIRE CANOE FINNEGAN

DENIS J. HARRINGTON
and
CHARLIE STEEL

Condor Publishing, Inc.
Lincoln, Michigan

FIRE CANOE FINNEGAN
by Denis J. Harrington and Charlie Steel

November 2015

Library of Congress Control Number: 2015956665

ISBN-13: 978-1-931079-12-9

Condor Publishing, Inc.
PO Box 39
123 S. Barlow Road
Lincoln, MI 48742
www.condorpublishinginc.com

Cover: Snags (im Missouri versunkene Baumstämme)
by Karl Bodmer
Image provided through the courtesy of
www.OldBookArt.com

Printed in the United States of America

This book is dedicated to all the brave steamboat captains who traversed the great rivers of the west.

D.J.H.

And to Denis J. Harrington whose vision made this book possible.

C.S.

In the spring of 1866, the guns of the War Between the States could no longer be heard. But this conflict, which so divided the land, still resonated in many hearts on both sides of the Mason-Dixon Line. And needless to say, the emotional wounds it inflicted would heal much more slowly than those which were suffered in the flesh.

Yet even the most devout advocates of the blue and the gray were able to close ranks in relative harmony to undertake the great task of settling and developing the uncharted expanse that unfolded west of the Mississippi and Missouri Rivers. Having put aside their military uniforms, these erstwhile enemies assumed the guise of farmers, cattlemen, trappers, prospectors, and railroaders as well as enterprising speculators and opportunists of all stripes.

Many of them set forth with bright expectations of what riches they hoped to find. For the most part these hardy adventurers were faced with unadvertised hardships, disillusionment, and death. The elements proved to be harsh and unforgiving as did the Indians native to the area, who deeply resented the intrusion into what was their land and private hunting ground. Western expansion meant treaties were not honored, and Native Americans facing constant depredation were forced to fight back as best they could in an attempt to save their lives and way of life.

Despite such impediments, there was no lack of enthusiasm for taking on the settlement of the West. The predominant Oregon and California Trails with their endless wagon trains became the expansive gateway to the Pacific Ocean. So it was that some of these adventurers crowded the decks of the steamboats which crossed the waters of the Mississippi and the Missouri Rivers to set out in quest of fame, fortune, and a new beginning. This account specifically focuses upon those men who piloted the steamers to various jumping-off places, who were no less resolute in their historic endeavors to conquer the west.

Here is a saga based on the likes of Captains Joseph Marie La Barge, Grant Marsh, the Charles Blunts (senior and junior), Daniel Maratta and William "Billy" Sims and their big, unwieldy boats that belched smoke (fire canoes) who, by means of guile and invention, managed to forge through sandbar-infested shallows and withstand capricious currents swirling with hull-rending snags and ice floes as a matter of course. Such men didn't reach the shores of the Pacific Ocean, but rather traveled the navigable rivers deep into the heart of the west, providing transportation and carrying men and supplies into dangerous territory.

These hardy steamboat pilots faced the dangers of killer storms, sudden tornadoes, Indian war parties, bands of roving thieves, and herds of migrating buffalo. While on board there was always the threat of boiler explosions, flash fires, mutiny, killings, and deadly diseases which frequently infected passengers as well as the crew in epidemic proportions.

Such events and developments as appear in this book define a different and rarer historical account of the settlement of the west: one that is a most memorable era in the saga of a nation rising.

CHAPTER ONE

With a rush of rippling water the small flatboat carrying its carefully wrapped supplies slipped around a sharp bend of the shoreline. The sunlit spires of St. Louis hove into view as the five men poled the boat closer to the shore. The city's levee was a clutter of colorful steamboats nosed into the line of docks like so many suckling pigs at feeding time.

Clint Finnegan took in the view, a surge of excitement welling up at the sight of the many steamboats. He began poling with more vigor. Strong muscles played along the length of his arms. He was anxious to reach land.

"Right pretty sight, ain't it?" observed a voice from over his shoulder.

"Yes, it is."

Finnegan glanced at the weathered face of his long time boss, master boatman Adas Werrtle.

"A lot doing there," the old man said, his dark, recessed eyes squinting into the glare of the sun. "St. Louis serves as a jumping off place for all kinds of folks heading west. Some of them would cut out a man's heart for the price of a drink."

Finnegan grinned. "I can see after myself."

"Never crossed my mind that you couldn't, my good friend," Werrtle replied with a shrug. "Just offering a word of advice."

"I appreciate the warning, sure enough."

A long-stem pipe was clenched between the old man's yellowed teeth.

"Sold everything, did you?" he inquired.

"Uh-huh." Finnegan's expression sobered. "The boat, the land, the house, and such as was in it."

"How did you fare, if I might ask?"

"Close to five hundred dollars."

A plume of smoke escaped the thin line of Werrtle's lips. "You done well," he remarked.

Finnegan made no response, all the while continuing to pole with strong, steady thrusts. He stood a bit over six feet and was thickly built. Blue eyes were set in a lean, sharply sculpted face, bronzed by exposure to the elements. A shock of unruly red hair crowned his austere features. He was not handsome, but women never failed to give him a second look.

"Keeping your fortune close at hand, I should hope," Werrtle remarked casually.

"To be certain." Finnegan gestured in the direction of a carpetbag situated nearby. Stretched out beside the bag was a large dog with a blunt, protruding jaw. "Duke stands watch for me."

Werrtle studied the animal for a time.

"Of a truth, the dog's enough to turn any soul from straying," he stated in a matter-of-fact manner. "But a money belt would be safer."

"I'll be getting one first thing," Finnegan responded.

Knocking ashes from his pipe, Werrtle said, "Won't change your mind about leaving?"

"Nope. As much as I hate to, old man, it's time for me to move along."

"Gonna have to tie up permanent some day."

"I know. But it's got to be the right place."

"How do you figure to tell?" Werrtle persisted.

Finnegan shook his head. "Guess it'll just come onto me."

The other three temporary hired hands lounged near the stern of the flatboat, long poles held idly in their strong hands. Every so often they would break off their conversation to cast sidelong glances at Finnegan. Werrtle hailed them with a motion of his arm.

"All right, lads, let's put our backs to it," he said. "We want to dock before dark."

The men lifted their poles, put them in the water, and began pushing the flatboat along. One of them, tall and burly, with a livid scar across the bridge of his nose, leaned close to his nearest companion and whispered, "The money's stowed in that bag. It's ours for the taking."

"What about the hound?" the man replied, eying the ever-vigilant dog.

"You don't think I got more brains than a dumb mutt?"

"Now, now, Mitch, I didn't mean nothin like ..."

"Bend to it now, lads," Werrtle interjected. "Bend to it. The current will be getting stronger soon."

Mitch nodded to the others and they put their weight to the poles. Finnegan paused in his efforts to stare in awe at the collection of stern and side-wheel steamboats which were moored at the pier only a few yards away.

"I've never seen them up close," he said quietly. "They're a whole lot bigger than I thought."

"They are." Werrtle removed his pipe and used it to point out one of the double-deck craft. "Take that one right there, the Mississippi Belle. She measures a good one hundred and seventy feet, and can carry upwards of two hundred tons through knee-deep water without so much as scraping her hull."

"That's something all right." Finnegan's gaze roamed the configuration of the riverboat from the jut of the fore spar to the twin smokestacks and on along the passenger deck to the tiller arm of the stern wheel. "Never seen the like of it."

"She's got two steam engines that can turn that big wheel twenty times a minute," Werrtle continued. "If you're traveling the river, there's nothing at all like it."

"How come you know so much about them?" asked Finnegan.

"Worked aboard them before the war," Werrtle replied. "Had my cap set to become a pilot one day." A sad expression seemed to deepen the lines that quilted the old man's face. He spit into the swirling waters. "But the Yankee what shot me through the leg at Vicksburg flat done away with all that business. There's just not much call for a cripple in the wheel house of a wide-river steamer."

"I'm real sorry about it, Master Werrtle."

"All a man can do is play the cards the way they fall." He gestured toward an opening between a couple of the big boats. "Looks like as good a place as any. We'll put in there."

Dark was quickly descending when Finnegan finished knotting the line of the flatboat to a piling and stepped back onto the deck. The three men stood aft in a tight cluster as Werrtle went to meet them.

"Here you be, lads," he said handing each of them a small sack. "You should count it careful now."

Coins clinked softly as deft fingers methodically verified the allotted amount. At length the three men pocketed their wages and came forward.

"Finnegan don't plan on returning to New Orleans with us, fellas," Werrtle announced. "He'll be going west to seek his fortune."

"Well, you don't say." A mirthless smile wormed its way across the full lips of the man called Mitchel. "It's sad we are to see you cast off," he said, nodding to his companions. "Ain't that so, gents?"

"To be sure," one of them responded. "You gonna take to farming?"

Finnegan shook his head. "I've got no ambition to get behind a plow." He smiled easily and watched the three step off the boat. "The best to you all," he called.

When the men were lost to view in the shadows of the wharf, Werrtle said, "They ain't among your admirers."

"You noticed that too?"

"I'd keep a sharp watch fore and aft so long as they're in port." Werrtle held out a small sack of coins. "Your wages. Better count it."

"No need for me to do so." Finnegan slipped the money inside his jacket.

Werrtle's worn features expressed disapproval.

"I wish you weren't so trusting, son," he remarked quietly. "Plenty of folks out there willing to take advantage."

"Yes, I know, but not you." Finnegan glanced around him. "Who'll be staying with the cargo tonight?"

"Me." Werrtle lifted his pullover to reveal a holstered gun. "I got this sidearm handy and have a resting place under them canvases." He gestured to where a small mound of packing crates were lashed to the deck. "Come tomorrow afternoon my buyers will be here and the sales made. Then I'll set about finding a load for the trip back to New Orleans."

Nodding, Finnegan looked away.

Werrtle picked up a lantern, lifted the glass, struck a Lucifer, and lit the wick.

"I figured to buy you supper and a drink or two in town," Finnegan said. "Doesn't seem right for old friends to part with nothing more than a handshake."

For several moments Werrtle stared at the flickering lantern.

"Can't say I've ever been one to shun a feed," he replied in a measured tone. "If Duke will stand guard a spell, I'll be pleased to accept your offer."

"Done." Finnegan squatted beside the dog. "You stay here, Duke, and don't let anybody come aboard. When I get back you'll have something real tasty to chew on. How's that sound?"

The big mongrel whimpered softly, his tail rhythmically thumping the deck.

Carpetbag in hand, Finnegan accompanied Werrtle across the levee in the direction of the illuminated storefronts. The buildings showed brightly against the clear night sky.

"It looks like a picture from one of those fancy calendars," Finnegan observed.

Werrtle nodded. "Hard to believe all this was burned to a cinder less than twenty years ago."

"Seems I remember hearing about that."

"Back in 1849 they had one God-awful fire right about where we're standing," Werrtle explained. "It started down at the dock." He indicated the area from which they had just come. "The flames leaped from one ship to another, and then the wind blew the fire inland. And before they could put it out, the whole waterfront was lost."

"You were here then?" said Finnegan.

"Nope. Only we passed by a few days later. It beat anything I ever saw."

They walked on. The sidewalk fronting the glut of supply stores, cheap eateries, and a variety of saloons was alive with a mix of riverboat people and locals. Laughter and singing spilled out into the street from a succession of open doorways. Finnegan and Werrtle paused to survey their surroundings.

"Less than a block from here is a hotel," Werrtle remarked. "The food there ain't half bad and there's plenty of it. You game?"

"Just about anything would be welcome right now," Finnegan said.

With Werrtle showing the way, they proceeded along the bustling walk, unaware that they were being followed. Some distance behind, Mitch and his two companions kept pace.

When they arrived at the hotel, Werrtle went into the restaurant and Finnegan remained before the clerk's desk to rent a room. There were several customers waiting in line ahead of him and it took a long twenty minutes before he completed his task.

Displaying an unsteady hand, Werrtle poured more of the bright amber liquid into his glass, then sat back to sip it. He was caught up in an intoxicated reverie.

Finnegan returned to the table and seated himself, sadly noting the old man's condition.

"Get settled, did you?" Werrtle questioned thickly.

"Yes. The room's a mite small, but the bed is nice and soft."

"What you got in mind to do?"

"For the time being, I just plan to head west," Finnegan replied with some hesitation. "Go as far as I can, then see what presents itself."

"How are you gonna get there?" Werrtle probed.

"While in line for a room, I had time to read. There's all kinds of notices for hire posted in the lobby," Finnegan replied. "Everybody's looking for a little extra muscle. And I can shoot and live off the land as well as the next fella."

"You make a good river man," Werrtle said. "I think you're plum touched in the head to go out there. By the time you've come to your senses, it may be much too late. Your money could be all gone and it won't be easy to find a way back. Then what?"

Finnegan frowned and remained silent for a time.

"I love the river as much as you do, Master Werrtle," he responded at length, choosing his words carefully. "But it's not taking me anywhere."

"How do you mean?"

"What can I look forward to—a life poling a flatboat?"

The old man's face evinced the hurt he felt inside.

Finnegan could have kicked himself. "I…I meant no disrespect," he stammered.

"You ain't been the same since the war," Werrtle said in a barely audible voice. "What happened, Clint?"

"Guess I got a whole lot different notions about... things..." Finnegan avoided looking at the old man. "And about myself."

"I don't follow you, son."

"Before the war I was content to do what Dad had always done, work the bayous and sell the skins upriver." Finnegan stared into space, his mind retreating through the years. "Even as a boy I could kill and strip gators, snakes and otters with the best. I knew how to handle a canoe and do all the bargaining with the shippers. And I got used to being alone for long periods of time. To be flat honest, I kind of liked the solitude. On those days when the sun came filtering through the trees and danced on the still water like so many diamonds, I was in a world all my own. I loved that world. But once the fighting started, everything changed."

Werrtle nodded his assent. "To be sure," he agreed softly.

"Instead of killing animals, I learned to kill men," Finnegan continued in a soft voice. "Whenever there would be bodies beside the road I would stop to study the faces. Kind of wondered who they were; if they had left loved ones behind. On occasion there would be among them someone from my unit. And all my questions would be answered."

Again Werrtle nodded his assent. Finnegan paused to pour himself a little whiskey.

"They assigned me to a cavalry outfit and I grew to like it," he began anew. "What's more—I liked having responsibility. Not only for myself, but others as well. I found out I could lead and men would follow."

"I could have guessed that about you," Werrtle said.

"Planning, strategy, map reading; it all came to me as easy as snapping my fingers. By the time the war ended I had the command of a captain. And if I had been a Yankee instead of a Reb, I'd be an officer and a gentlemen even now. Who can say how far I might have gone?"

His head bowed, Werrtle said, "Your pa and me growed up together. And we worked on the river together. I never married, so he and your ma and you was family. Then he up and died and she went to live with her folks in Georgia. So I kind of stepped in your daddy's shoes, so far as you was concerned."

"And I'm most grateful that you did," said Finnegan.

"My war experiences weren't the same as yours," Werrtle interjected. "And I reckon that's because I got wounded early. I can't say I really fault you for wanting to go west. Probably do the same if I was young and unfettered." He shook his head as though dazed. "A man can get powerful silly when he's old. Swore I'd never drink this much, but I went and did it anyway."

They sat without a word passing between them for what seemed an eternity. Werrtle finally lurched to his feet.

"Best be getting back to the boat," he said, leaning heavily on his chair.

Finnegan lent a steadying hand to his friend.

"I can navigate, be it fair weather or fowl," Werrtle insisted, attempting to walk on his own.

"Tell you what," Finnegan said. "Suppose I take the first watch. You can sleep in my room. I'll come for you just before sunrise. You'll need to be fresh for tomorrow. It's going to be a busy day."

"Uh, well that might be best," Werrtle conceded lethargically.

"Come on, let's get you to bed."

Finnegan helped an unsteady Werrtle to the hotel lobby and then up an adjoining staircase. When they were lost to view, a man wearing the uniform of a steamboat captain approached the clerk at the registration desk.

"That young fellow who just passed here with the inebriated gentleman, could you give me his name?" the captain asked.

The clerk's eyes narrowed, "Can't say I noticed either of them."

With a knowing smile the captain retrieved a number of coins from a jacket pocket and laid them on the counter.

"Big, strong, with red hair," described the captain. "Think you might remember now?"

"Just so happens I do." The clerk consulted the hotel register. "The name's Finnegan. Clint Finnegan."

"All right, thank you."

"Is he in some kind of trouble?" the clerk questioned.

"Nothing of which I'm aware."

The captain returned to the dining room and seated himself at a table near the lobby. Before long Finnegan came down the stairs and moved to the registration desk.

"My friend will be using the room tonight," he told the clerk. "I'll be back in the morning to get my things."

Finnegan turned to leave, only to hear the clerk ask, "Who is the man taking your place?"

He made no response but took a pen from the counter, dipped it in the desk well, and scribbled in the registration book. The clerk considered the entry with a puzzled frown.

"Adas Werrtle," Finnegan said, and walked off.

No sooner had he left through the street door than the captain rose and followed. Despite the deserted appearance of the levee, Finnegan had the very distinct impression he was not alone. He stopped to look and listen. He saw nothing suspicious, but anyone could be hiding in the shadows of the many boats. Reflexively, he slipped a hand inside his jacket. The pouch containing his money was still securely in place. He began walking again. His thoughts turned to Werrtle's pistol and he silently berated himself for not having brought it along.

"Out kind of late ain't you, Clint?"

The unexpected sound of a voice brought him up short. It was as if the three men simply materialized out of the darkness. They confronted him, standing some distance apart. Immediately he took stock of the situation.

"Seems like a fella would have better sense than to tote all that money around on his lonesome."

Finnegan recognized the voice as belonging to Mitch.

"We'll just have to put it in a safe place," another of the men remarked. "Like in our pockets."

As they closed in, Finnegan slowly retreated, inwardly reviewing his options. Running would be senseless, he determined. And there was no use calling for help in such a place. So he had but one alternative—do the unexpected.

"Best fork over the money," Mitch said, "and save yourself a lot of grief."

"Guess...I don't...don't have much choice," Finnegan replied.

The men slowed their advance and Mitch held out his hand.

"Just give me the lot of it and you can go on your way."

"You expect me to believe that?" said Finnegan.

"Sure. You got my word on it."

Finnegan could sense them hesitating. He coolly sized up the man nearest him. Just as Clint prepared to lunge, Mitch spoke again.

"Better yet," he said, "just keep your hands where we can see them."

He motioned to one of his companions. "Take the money."

The man came up cautiously, the stale stench of tobacco and whiskey strong about him.

"Where you got it?" he demanded gruffly.

Finnegan pointed to the open neck of his shirt. As the man leaned close, a large fist slammed into his jaw. In an instant, his knees sagged and the thief was sent sprawling backward. He collapsed at Mitch's feet and lay still.

"You're just making it tough on yourself," Mitch growled.

The thief withdrew something from beneath the tail of his shirt and extended it in front of him. It was a thick-handled, wide-bladed knife.

"Let's do it, Curly," Mitch said.

The two men rushed forward.

Turning sideways, Finnegan ventured a vicious kick at his knife-wielding assailant and was rewarded with an agonizing howl. Mitch retreated, clutching his leg. Curly loomed large out of the gloom. Finnegan forced a forearm across the man's throat and was anointed with a shower of spittle. But the big man still managed to apply a bear-like embrace. Finnegan sunk his teeth into an available ear and the powerful arms that embraced him went limp. Now he grabbed his attacker's bushy beard and yanked down hard. In the same motion he brought a knee up sharply. There was a guttural grunt and the man fell like a toppled tree.

"Looks as though that leaves just you and me to contend over what's mine," Finnegan said.

"I'll carve it out of your hide," came the snarled reply.

From his earliest days on the New Orleans docks Finnegan had been known as a brawler with a thorough command of rough and tumble tactics. He could claw, bite, gouge, and butt with the best of them.

Mitch came on methodically out of a half crouch, prodding with the knife. Finnegan moved erratically from side to side, pausing intermittently for a well-placed kick to the knees. His objective was to goad Mitch into attacking recklessly. At length the tactic bore fruit.

With a savage thrust, Mitch directed the blade to his midsection. Finnegan deftly avoided the move and caught the outstretched arm in the crook of his elbow. He twisted hard. Mitch gave a yelp and relinquished the knife to the damp stones underfoot.

In desperation, Mitch went for Finnegan's eyes with the fingers of his free hand. But the attack was blocked. While they wrestled for advantage, their breath exploded in forceful gasps. Curly slowly raised himself to all fours. Just a few yards away lay the fallen knife. He crawled toward it, his eyes fixed on Finnegan's back. Blade now in hand, he gained his feet and crept forward. As he was poised to strike, a gunshot sounded. He pirouetted awkwardly on the balls of his feet. Then another shot rang out and he slumped to the ground.

From the neighboring shadows stepped the steamboat captain. He briefly considered his handiwork before returning a revolver to its place inside his jacket. Then he waited with arms crossed for the combatants to settle their disagreement.

Finnegan could feel Mitch's strength beginning to ebb. He promptly took advantage of the situation by circling his arms, picking up his adversary, and applying a steely bear hug. Mitch groaned in distress and tried to knee his tormenter in the groin but was roughly jerked off balance before he could succeed. Then the top of Finnegan's head struck Mitch forcefully under the chin. The assailant went down with a thud, his unprotected face bouncing off the ragged stones. He lay there motionless.

"You did yourself proud," the captain remarked.

Finnegan peered into the darkness at the indistinct figure. Then he turned around to view the bodies of the fallen. "I heard shooting; was it you?"

"It was." The captain gestured toward Curly's inert form and the knife still in his grasp. "He was about to run you through."

"Much obliged," Finnegan said. "I didn't really expect anyone to be around this time of night."

"Oh I wasn't here by chance. I followed you from the hotel."

Finnegan frowned. "You followed me?'

"Yes, I overheard your conversation with the old man in the dining room. You talked about going out west. I sized you up and thought you might be interested in a proposition that could change the course of your life. So how about it?"

Given a moment's contemplation, Finnegan responded, "Well, seeing you saved my life, the least I can do is hear what you have to say."

"I would appreciate it." The captain held out his hand. "My name is Shadloe Glazer. I'm in command of a steamboat called the Dakota Dawn. For the past couple of years I've been hauling both passengers and cargo up the Missouri River. We make such stops as Fort Randall, Cow Island, and as far north as Fort Buford. Ever been to the territories?"

Finnegan shook his head. "This is my first trip this far north."

"I see," Glazer said. "My ship is moored not far from here. If you'll come along with me, I promise to spell out everything in short order. Then a simple yes or no will do. Fair enough?"

"Sure thing." Finnegan jerked a thumb in the direction of the prostrate ambushers. "But what about them?"

"The dock patrol will be around come morning," Glazer replied. "I don't believe they would have thought twice about leaving you to lay face down."

"I suppose you're right."

With that they went off together to the main dock. Aboard the steamship, Glazer unlocked his cabin door. In the glare of the desk lamp, Finnegan got his first good look at the captain. He was of slight build and immaculately turned out in his uniform. The flesh of his face seemed unusually pale and contrasted sharply with a dark, neatly clipped mustache, and sideburns. His hazel eyes were steady and penetrating. Finnegan towered over him and was a much broader figure.

"If the hotel register is to be believed, your name is Clint Finnegan," he said in a slow, deliberate manner. "True?"

"Yes sir, it is."

"There is one matter which I feel ought to be addressed from the very outset," Glazer explained. "And that is I'm a Yankee. I served with the Union during the hostilities and would do so again if it became necessary. Should this be a stumbling block between us, then I thank you for your patience."

Finnegan considered how much Glazer seemed like an undersized gamecock. He could have plucked his feathers without much trouble. And he felt certain this fact had occurred to the little captain as well. But the man did save his life and to that extent Finnegan was indebted to him.

"I've got no quarrel with your convictions," Finnegan replied. "Seems enough folks have died over that difference of opinion."

"Quite so, quite so. Were you involved in the fighting?"

"Here and there."

"On the side of the gray, I presume?"

"Correct."

"What was your outfit?" Glazer inquired. "Just wondered if our paths might have crossed during the conflict."

"Mosby's Raiders."

"Ah, you were a cavalry man."

"That's right."

"May I inquire as to your rank?"

"Captain, at the cessation of hostilities. It was a field commission."

"I see." Glazer thought a moment before adding, "An officer and a gentleman by promotion."

"Did my best. How about you?"

"Charged with gunnery aboard a federal warship on the Mississippi."

"Your rank?"

"Major." Glazer smiled. "We made any number of runs against the Confederate fortifications at Memphis as well as Vicksburg."

Finnegan nodded. "Never got over that way myself. But I know folks who did. Just so much history now. And a good thing it is, if you ask me."

"I heartily agree." Glazer unrolled what appeared to be a hand-drawn map and spread it across the table. "This is a somewhat crude rendition of how the Missouri River flows down from the new territories. Nonetheless, I've found it sufficiently accurate for navigation purposes. I've been through the area enough to have recorded all the necessary details."

Finnegan watched a finger trace the length of the waterway's winding configuration.

"The lower end of the river is deep," Glazer said, "but up north rock beds, snags, shifting sandbars, and floating debris will tear the guts right out of most steamers. The Dakota Dawn can float upwards of three hundred and fifty tons while displacing less than two feet of water. She's the vanguard of the future—the kind of craft to take men and materials to the head of the Missouri and its tributaries. The smaller rivers crisscross the territories from one end to the other. They're the real routes to the west—certainly for past explorers and the fur trade."

"Can't say I ever thought of it that way," Finnegan said.

Glazer paused, then he set about detailing the danger of water travel into the northwest.

"Gales, thunderstorms and tornadoes coming off the land will sink a steamboat faster than you can blink," he said. "During the winter, ice floes are a danger. In the summer months, migrating buffalo will come across your deck and wind-blown sparks from a prairie fire can finish you right quickly. Epidemics among the passengers and crew, as well as exploding boilers, are a problem year round. And if this isn't enough there's always the threat of boarding parties, both Indians and river bandits. You've got to handle a gun and a knife with equal facility. This isn't a business for the faint of heart."

"Certainly doesn't sound like it," Finnegan replied. "So what's your proposition?"

"I need a stout, honest man to apprentice as assistant master," Glazer explained. "Which means you will be helping load the boilers, make repairs of all kinds, take charge of the crew, settle disputes among the passengers, and fight to protect the ship should the occasion arise. I'll teach you to pilot the river as time allows. But most of the learning will come through doing. My experience is you either have a feel for steering or you don't."

"And the pay?" Finnegan questioned.

"Twenty dollars a month plus food and quarters."

"Can't say that's much for all the grief you describe."

His voice assuming a confidential tone, Glazer said, "Before the war I started as a crew member. I worked my way up to captain. When the war started they made me a major and I'm not thirty as yet. What's more, I own part of the Dakota Dawn. Within a few years I'll be sitting behind a desk while other people pilot my boats." He leaned closer. "I didn't have any more going for me than you do—maybe less, given your experience working on a flatboat."

Finnegan was never one to buy snake oil. But he did know a thing or two about river boating. And he was in the market for an opportunity with a future. Visions of him in the wheelhouse of the Dakota Dawn flashed through his mind. *Master Werrtle said there is nothing quite like sailing the big steamers. So why not take the challenge? I have nothing to lose. Or do I?*

"I'd be interested to know what happened to the last assistant master?" Finnegan inquired.

"A boiler blew up and he went with it," came the terse response. "And before him the Indians got a few and some others just quit. Well, what do you say?"

"Guess I'll give it a try," Finnegan replied after some hesitation. "So when do I start?"

"At noon tomorrow. Our important destination is the army garrison at Cow Island. At various times we'll be putting in at St. Joseph, Fort Randall, Nebraska City, Bismark, and even Fort Buford, in the

Dakota Territory. As a matter of fact, when we need wood, we'll be making a number of unscheduled stops. Most of the time we'll be buying wood and when we can't, we'll scavage where we can. The cargo is a mix of food stuffs and mining equipment as well as assorted textiles. And there will be a few passengers as well."

"What goes to the Cow Island garrison?"

"An army payroll."

"The army will have a guard detail?" Finnegan asked.

"Yes. Caring for the money will be strictly their responsibility."

"When should I report?"

"Be aboard by ten o'clock," Glazer replied. "That will give you a few hours to settle your personal affairs in the morning."

"I appreciate it."

They shook hands and Glazer led the way to the promenade deck. En route, Finnegan gazed up at the twin smokestacks that loomed large overhead and felt a twinge of apprehension sweep through him.

At the stairs which went down to the main deck Glazer said," Just a word of advice. I wouldn't bring anything of value with you tomorrow. Odds are there will be trouble if you do."

"Don't worry. After what happened tonight I've learned my lesson."

Finnegan started down the stairs only to have Glazer's voice halt him.

"Mr. Finnegan."

"Yes?"

"I'll be relying very heavily on you in the days ahead," Glazer said. "So it's most important that we work closely together in an atmosphere of mutual trust. Our collective survival could hinge on how well we get along."

"I couldn't agree more," Finnegan replied. "You stepped in for me this evening, and you can count on me returning the favor if that ever becomes necessary. Just the way it should be between officers and gentlemen, right?"

"Precisely." Glazer saluted. "I see recruiting you was fortuitous indeed. Good night, Mr. Finnegan."

"Good night, sir," said Clint, returning the salute.

Upon reaching the levee, Finnegan paused to scan the imposing mass of the Dakota Dawn. His eyes moved from the fore spar and the jackstaff which jutted into the night sky like a great forbidding finger. Aft rose the huge paddlewheel with its iron struts. In a matter of just a few short hours, he mused, it would be churning the river waters to a white foam. He was plagued by doubts—nagging doubts—about his ability to do the task so quickly pressed upon him.

Back at the flatboat, Duke greeted his master by licking his face and wagging his tail. Finnegan emptied his pockets of the food scraps which had been acquired from the hotel dining room and he fed them to the big dog. Wearily, the tough southern veteran lit a lantern and stretched out on several meal sacks.

"We'll be heading up to the territories tomorrow, Duke, old boy," he said softly, "and I'm beginning to wonder if it's not a mistake. But, I've given my word. In the morning we'll get help poling the flatboat alongside the Dakota Dawn. She'll be safe there while we go to the bank. We'll wake up Werrtle on the way."

CHAPTER TWO

Finnegan took a quick look at the wall clock and hurriedly affixed his signature to the voucher slip and its duplicate. The bank manager sat back in his soft chair, a finger idly tracing the line of his mustache. He smelled of talcum and barbershop tonic.

"Does that do it?" Finnegan inquired, laying down the pen.

"Just one more thing," the manager replied. "You'll need to designate a beneficiary. Someone who may lawfully withdraw the monies deposited in the event you should die unexpectedly."

"Oh, yes." Finnegan turned to Werrtle. "I want that to be you, Adas."

Werrtle appeared to be uncomfortable.

"You sure?" he questioned.

"Very sure."

Werrtle nodded and picked up the pen. The bank manager indicated the lines on the forms to be completed. His expression grim, Werrtle set about the task as though he had been required to etch the information in stone. Several minutes passed before he was finished.

"Can you read it all right?" he inquired self-consciously.

The bank manager briefly studied the display of penmanship before replying, "Yes, this will do nicely."

"I ain't had much schooling," Werrtle explained, his manner apologetic, "so writing and such comes kind of hard for me."

Smiling blandly, the bank manager said, "I quite understand." Then he handed Finnegan a slip of paper. "Here is your receipt of deposit and your bank book. If I can be of any further service, please don't hesitate to call on me." So saying, he got to his feet and waited for the two patrons to leave.

Outside of the manager's office Finnegan and Werrtle paused to gaze at the furnishings of the bank lobby. Twin chandeliers were suspended from a vaulted ceiling which featured an elaborate mural that depicted the founding of St. Louis. Rows of burnished brass teller windows framed in dark mahogany lined one side of the large room. Along the thick carpeted center aisle were situated a number of glass-top writing tables as well as several upholstered arm chairs and a succession of tall, potted plants.

"Pretty fancy ain't it?" Werrtle observed.

"I should say," Finnegan responded.

They turned toward the street entrance where Finnegan had left Duke guarding his carpetbag. Reaching the sidewalk, they headed in the direction of the waterfront without a word passing between them. Parting would be difficult, and particularly so since they might not be seeing one another for some time. The leaden silence prevailed until they were standing at the gangway to the Dakota Dawn.

"You got yourself a real fine opportunity here," Werrtle said, his gaze roving the length of the massive steamboat. "A man can make a handsome fortune working one of these if he puts himself to it."

"So I hear," replied Finnegan.

Werrtle swallowed hard. "I'd give most anything to be going with you. But those days are over." He shook his head slowly. "Well, guess I better say God speed until next we meet, be it on this side or the other."

Making no reply, Finnegan gently but briefly hugged the old man.

"I'm … I'm going to miss you something fierce, Master Werrtle," he said with considerable effort.

"The same here, lad, but we're traveling different roads now. Mine's leveling off while yours is just winding upward." Werrtle paused to clear his throat. "Promise me you'll always do your best."

"I…I promise." Finnegan's voice was barely audible.

"Do that and you ain't never gonna be sorry," Werrtle said, then pivoted sharply and hobbled off.

Finnegan felt remorse at leaving the old man. It was then he heard Glazer calling to him from the main deck.

"Clint, I need you now," he said. "We'll be casting off soon."

"Yes sir." Finnegan went over to where Duke waited beside his belongings. "Come on, fella, we'll have to be going."

Together they boarded the steamer and followed a deck hand into the cargo hold.

A voice from across the room directed him. "Put in wherever you can, lad. Seems as though most everybody's taken a claim."

The speaker wore a gap-toothed grin that formed in the grizzled expanse of beard and he appeared to be friendly enough. He was a squat, muscular fellow with closely cropped gray hair. Surprisingly agile, the man sat cross-legged on the deck floor of the cargo hold, his broad back resting against a stanchion. A clay pipe was all but lost in the bulk of his fist.

"You're the new hand, I take it," he said.

Finnegan nodded.

"I go by Benjamin Watts."

"Clint Finnegan."

"Right happy to know you." Watts gestured toward Duke with the pipe. "Nice looking animal. Of civil disposition, is he?"

"Usually."

Finnegan deposited his belongings on the worn boards and surveyed the area. Blankets, chests, knapsacks and similar paraphernalia lay around in the places not occupied by cargo. There was even a hammock strung between the stanchions. He saw a single canoe and yawl boats hung down on either side of the very expansive space, which was without walls. At its far end were tethered three horses, and near them lay tack and three military saddles. Water lapped just a few feet below the floor level and intermittently a wind-whipped spray lent a chill to the atmosphere.

"Have you ever worked with Captain Glazer before?" Watts asked.

"No."

"One of the best masters on the river. Perhaps more than a little stiff in his demeanor but a good man round about."

"Been with him long?" Finnegan asked.

"Going on two years."

"And your position?"

"I feed the boilers and help out as needs be," Watts replied. "Yourself?"

Finnegan smiled.

"Like you, a little of everything."

"Worked steamers before, have you?" Watts persisted.

"Nope. Just flatboats."

Grinning, Watts continued, "Seeking adventure or perhaps a place in the wheelhouse?"

"I have it in mind to be a master some day."

"Noble ambition." Watts laughed hoarsely as though enjoying a private joke. "And all the adventure a man could want comes with it."

Suddenly there was a clanging of a bell and Watts scrambled to his feet.

"That's a call for all hands," he explained. "We're shoving off, I'll wager."

Finnegan made his way to mid deck to see several crew members rapidly assembling beside the boilers. A large black man was busily stoking the firebox, his bare torso glistening with perspiration. Watts hurried to join him. Steam rose out of the twin stacks in billowing columns as the engine started to move the tiller arm.

Glazer came out of the wheelhouse and shouted loudly, "All hands prepare to disengage."

Immediately two deckhands ran forward and began hauling aboard the heavy hawser that moored the ship to the pier. The remainder of the crew picked up long poles stored on the deck and used them to prod the hull clear of the levee. Finnegan knew this chore well and promptly took up a position near the bow and helped pole. Slowly they swung away into the drift of the river as the huge paddlewheel commenced to turn. Within a matter of a few minutes the powerful arms were churning the water astern, ever so steadily driving the ship into and against the current.

As the Dakota Dawn moved out onto the river, Finnegan scanned the receding levee until his gaze encountered a familiar flatboat. There stood Adas Werrtle watching the steamboat get underway, hat across his chest as though in mourning. Finnegan began to wave a final parting salute, then thought better of it. Leave well enough alone, he decided. Returning the pole to the deck, he wondered what would be required of him next. Surely an assistant master just didn't stand around unoccupied. Then there were strong fingers on his shoulder.

"You Finnegan?"

His inquisitor wore a bright red bandana about his head. Sprigs of hair bleached white by the sun protruded indiscriminately. The face beneath was full, bearded and ruddy, with deep-set eyes as dull as slate. Not an amicable mix by any measure. But the nose is what fixed Finnegan's attention. It was flat with flared nostrils. He had seen the like on professional barge fighters who plied their trade along the New Orleans bayous. The broad-knuckled hand relinquished its hold.

"That's right," Finnegan replied.

"Captain wants to see you." The man raised an arm thick as a wagon tongue to indicate the wheelhouse. "Right now."

Finnegan nodded. He didn't care for the tone of the man's voice. It denoted a belligerent nature and the prospect of trouble down the line.

"I hear tell you're the new assistant master," the man said.

"Yes?"

"Well that don't mean nothin' to Will Scower." He tapped his chest with a battered thumb. "Will Scower does as he sees fit." So saying, he sauntered off.

Finnegan watched him go. The messenger was barrel-chested and wide shouldered but moved with a deceptive ease. All these things Finnegan contemplated en route to the wheelhouse. Once there, he stood outside the glass paneled door until beckoned to enter.

"Get settled?" Glazer inquired, his eyes remaining on the river.

"Yes sir."

"Meet the rest of the crew?"

"Some of them."

"That'll pretty well take care of itself." Glazer motioned toward the cluttered table nearby. "Open that packet there and take out the map from inside."

It was a polished leather carrying case with an impressive brass buckle. Finnegan worked the overlying strap free and lifted the heavy flap to expose a folded sheet of waxen paper. He carefully extended it atop the table.

"No doubt you've done considerable map reading," Glazer said.

"Yes sir."

"That's a more detailed version of the one you saw last night," Glazer said. "It's got every nook and cranny of the river on it from here to Camp Buford, up where the Dakota and Montana territories come together. I marked all the shallows, sandbars, the rapids and the like. That's not to suggest things can't change but at least one knows where to be on the lookout."

"Yes sir."

"See the little box at the lower right hand corner?"

"Yes sir."

"That's the key. It deciphers all those signs on the map. One kind of line means sandbars, another kind means rapids and so on. I'm sure you'll learn everything easy enough."

"Yes sir."

Glazer glanced over his shoulder. "I want you to take the map below tonight and study it until you've got every detail firmly in mind. Can you do that?"

"I believe so."

There was a moment of silence before he added, "I'm counting on you, Clint. Really counting on you. Before this trip is over, everything might come down to how well you learned that map."

"Expecting trouble?"

More silence ensued.

"Let's just say that I'm a very cautious man, especially when I've got an army payroll on board."

"Don't you think the guard detail can handle things?"

"Yes. But you still have to be ready for the unexpected."

Finnegan had always liked maps. As a boy he studied those contained in the leatherbound book his father kept on the kitchen shelf. Then came those which were stacked on a stand behind his teacher's desk. Maps meant faraway places and adventure to him. After going over them time and again he would close his eyes and dream about traveling to exotic lands. Years later he scrutinized maps by candlelight while huddled with his horse in barren fields and shattered woods. With the maps, he followed the Union troops' every movement. Now he intended to become a close observer of the river.

"You can put that away and come over here," Glazer said with a wave of his hand.

When Finnegan had secured the packet once again, he was directed to take the wheel.

"You...you want me to...steer?" he stammered in disbelief.

Glazer grinned. "How else do you expect to learn?"

To Finnegan's surprise, the wheel moved easily in his grasp.

"Palms down on either side," Glazer instructed, "and keep a sharp eye out for anything that might cross your bow."

"Last night you mentioned something about migrating buffalo."

"Sure as your life," Glazer replied. "More than once I've seen a herd of buffalo cross the water. And they don't stop for anything."

"What's to be done then?"

"Just miss as many of them as possible without going aground. You can't stop and wait because there are so many of them, it may take two hours or more for them to make the swim. No matter how hard you try, some of them are going to be killed. Such mishaps sure rile the Indians."

"Am I supposed to guide on something?"

"When piloting straight ahead, line your jackstaff up with the bow. So long as there's room, stay a healthy distance from the two shore banks," Glazer explained. "When the river narrows you've got to keep centered so as not to bottom out. And it's no easy task when the current's against you."

"What's that?" Finnegan indicated a length of cord hanging through an opening in the ceiling.

"An attachment to a steam whistle situated on the wheelhouse roof," Glazer explained. "You usually pull it to warn off other vessels should they be running starboard to your course. On occasion it can be a distress signal."

Finnegan pointed to a cable which was attached to the base of the wheel. "And this?"

"That's our lifeline."

Finnegan looked puzzled. "Lifeline?"

"Yes indeed," Glazer affirmed. "It stretches to the stern and controls the tiller arm of the rudder. Should it break, we couldn't steer the ship. We'd be at the mercy of the elements. Had it happen to me on one occasion. I ended up running a sandbar and tearing a hole in the hull."

"Did you sink?"

"No, we dumped our cargo," Glazer replied. "It cost the company a good twenty thousand dollars. Only blemish on my record." The captain lapsed into a prolonged silence before remarking, "I expect trouble on this trip."

Glancing over, Finnegan found Glazer staring pensively upriver, and made no response.

"I've carried payroll before," the captain began anew, "but I have a feeling about this one."

"Is there something in particular that bothers you?" Finnegan inquired, keeping his eyes straight ahead.

"The man I sent to get you, Will Scower. He's a bad sort. You're probably wondering why I hired him."

"Have to say I am," Finnegan replied.

"I had no choice really. My regular steersman turned up missing last night. He wasn't at the hotel when I went to meet him for dinner. And he didn't report for duty this morning. But Scower did." Glazer thumped a hand against the wall of the wheelhouse. "I'll give Scower his due," he said. "The man's as good as there is when it comes to handling the wheel. Only you simply can't trust him. He'd sell his mother for a swallow of cheap whiskey."

"Quite frankly, I don't see how he could go for the army payroll with that guard detail around," said Finnegan.

"Still, I don't like it," Glazer persisted. "My steersman disappears, then Scower just happens to be available. It's as though he knew I'd have to take him on."

"It's curious, all right."

"You appear to have a feel for steering," Glazer said, changing the subject.

"Well, I'm usually pretty able to learn on short notice," Finnegan replied. "And the sooner I get the hang of the wheel, the sooner you can get shed of Scower."

"Exactly what I had in mind," Glazer said. "I'll take over now. You had better go below and check the wood for the firebox. There's cord wood stored just forward of the cargo compartment."

"Yes sir."

As Finnegan opened the wheelhouse door to leave, Glazer added, "I forgot, you'll be eating with me and the passengers tonight in the dining room. I think it's better that everyone gets acquainted sooner rather than later. And you might be interested to learn that one of our guests is a very attractive young lady."

"Uh, well, I don't know if I'll cut much of a figure," Finnegan replied. "None of what I brought to wear is exactly Sunday-go-to-meeting."

Glazer chuckled. "Then just scrub up; maybe along the way you can purchase a jacket. After dinner we'll talk more in my cabin. And then I'll give you the map to study."

"When should I be there?"

"Six will do."

"Very well, sir."

The sun was warm on the nape of Finnegan's neck as he descended to the main deck. His mind was a jumble. Everything seemed to be happening much too fast. Inwardly he berated himself for having left Werrtle and the flatboat.

Buffalo gals, won't you come out tonight? Come out tonight, Come out tonight?

Buffalo gals, won't you come out tonight, and dance by the light of the moon.

The big tender sang in rich, base tones that defied the thunder of the boilers. He worked with powerful arms drenched in sweat and an almost serene expression across his handsome features. Alongside, Watts stoked as well, his face a study in contemplation.

Finnegan approached the two men and got Watts' attention.

"Need any wood?" he shouted over the din.

"We could do with another lot," Watts bellowed.

"I'll fetch some," said Finnegan.

With the stem of his pipe Watts pointed to a canvas sling hanging from a nearby wood crib and indicated that it should be draped over one shoulder for carrying purposes. Finnegan retrieved it and hurried forward, more than happy to be away from the noise of the boilers. As he walked along the deck, a feminine voice halted him.

"Hello there."

Stopping, Finnegan looked up to see a young woman on the stairs, leaning out at a precarious angle.

"Best be careful, ma'am," he cautioned. "You could take a nasty tumble."

"I'm really quite all right," she replied with a mischievous smile. "Do you know where I might find Captain Glazer?"

"He's in the wheelhouse, ma'am. Can I be of help?"

"I just had a question." She considered him closely. "Who are you, may I ask?"

"Clint Finnegan is the name."

He raised his hand as a shield against the glare. She was pretty. Very pretty. Soft brown curls wreathed her face. Delicately molded features held dark inquisitive eyes and full lips. He was vaguely aware of his pulse accelerating.

"Are you a ship's officer?"

"Uh, no ma'am."

"Would you know if there's a telegraph station anywhere between here and Fort Leavenworth?"

"No, ma'am. But I'll be glad to inquire of the captain, if you like."

"That won't be necessary." She smiled again, this time more warmly. "However, I do appreciate the offer, Mr. Finnegan."

Just as suddenly as she appeared, she was gone. He lingered for a few moments, still staring upward. Then, in something of a daze, he continued on and a loud voice reached his ears. When his vision became accustomed to the deepening shadows of the hold, he saw Scower confronting someone. He stepped inside for a better vantage point.

"It ain't enough for a Negro to be aboard," Scower roared, "but now we've got to bunk down with a savage."

The deck hands sat around, feigning an unconcerned air. Only the nervous glances which passed between them spoke volumes. Attending the three army horses was an Indian wearing a buckskin shirt and leggings. He was tall and lean but thick through the shoulders and flat of waist. His hands, which were polishing a cavalry saddle, were large, and forearms fairly rippled with sinew. A thick stand of jet black hair fell to the nape of his neck. His features displayed a calm, almost amused expression.

"Let's face it, we're gonna have to sleep with one eye open," Scower continued, "if we don't want to wake up missing our scalp."

"That's enough," Finnegan said quietly.

Swinging around, Scower grinned malevolently.

"Well lookee here, boys," he said. "It's our new assistant master. Real pretty, ain't he?"

There was no reaction from the others.

His manner changing, Scower growled, "Would you be calling me out, Finnegan?"

"Whatever is your pleasure."

Finnegan let the wood sling slip from his shoulder. Quiet settled over the cavernous hold. The two men locked gazes until, with a sneer, Scower turned away, his mumbled remark barely audible.

"I'll see to you and that savage in my own good time."

When Scower had gone, Finnegan went over to the Indian and smiled. He started to speak and then hesitated, not sure if his words would be understood.

"Creek understands English very well," the Indian said with a deep voice.

"I'm Clint Finnegan. You a scout with the army group?"

The Indian nodded. "Do you paddle this fire canoe?"

"So to speak," Finnegan replied. "Fire canoe is what your people call a steamboat?"

"Yes." Creek inclined his head to one side and grinned. "I'll call you Fire Canoe Finnegan."

Finnegan laughed easily. "All right, if you say so."

"The man with the caved-in nose, he hates you now," Creek added solemnly.

"I know. And he feels the same way about you."

"We both need to keep watch."

"You're right about that." Finnegan retrieved the wood sling and went out.

CHAPTER THREE

Finnegan's chin was tender to the touch. The lack of warm water and a dull razor were responsible for the discomfort. But it had no bearing on the sense of dread that filled him. He tugged at the wrinkles in his shirt. If given a choice, he would gladly have wrestled a bear rather than be required to eat dinner with Glazer and his passengers.

For certain, Finnegan wanted to make the acquaintance of the young woman. However, he quailed at the thought she might find him crude or worse yet, uninteresting. The knob to the door of the cabin dining room gave way grudgingly in his grasp. Four sets of kerosene lamps hung down from the ceiling rafters, brightening a long table adorned with a white cloth and glass plates. Glittering utensils wrapped in napkins marked each place, and silver bowls emitting vapors from beneath their lids completed the setting. At the far end of the compartment Glazer and four men sat around a potbelly stove, smoking and conversing. Two of them wore the uniform of the Union Army.

"Ah, Clint, there you are," Glazer said. "Come join us."

The captain beckoned and rose from his chair. The other men gazed intently as Finnegan approached. He felt very uncomfortable.

"Gentlemen, meet Clint Finnegan, my assistant master," Glazer said.

Eyes looked him up and down.

"I'm Hiram Butler, Clint."

A robust, graying man with full sideburns and a drooping mustache extended a hand.

"My pleasure, sir," Finnegan replied.

"This is Alonzo Winthrup," Glazer said gesturing to a second man. "He and Mr. Butler are business partners."

Winthrup was younger and more solidly built than his associate. He had sandy hair and freckles. A thin scar ran the length of his jaw. Cigar smoke veiled a pair of hazel eyes. He merely nodded.

The junior of the two officers got to his feet.

"Lieutenant Farris Harbaugh," he said crisply, an even row of teeth visible beneath a carefully manicured mustache. He was dark complected and well groomed. His uniform fit as though it were molded to his slight frame.

"And this is Major Avril Brunston," Glazer concluded.

"Howdy, Clint."

Brunstron leaned forward to present his hand. The fingers and the palm were heavily callused and the grip was strong. Both his hair and mustache were turning gray.

Just then the cabin door swung back and a young woman entered the room. She wore a black dress tightly tailored to her trim, athletic figure. Delicate lace encircled her throat; her gown seemed to gleam under the overhead lights. *Pretty just isn't the word,* Finnegan thought. *She is beautiful.* Her hair was swept into a mound of curls that were held tightly back by a dark ribbon. She moved gracefully.

"I'm very sorry to have kept you waiting, gentlemen," she said with a disarming smile.

"No inconvenience; no inconvenience whatsoever." Harbaugh moved quickly to her side. "May I say on behalf of us all that you look absolutely ravishing?"

"Thank you."

"You've met everyone here, Miss Parkinson," Glazer said, "with the exception of my assistant master."

"Clint Finnegan, I believe," she stated.

Harbaugh frowned. "You know each other?"

"We had occasion to speak earlier today," she replied, turning again to Finnegan. "My given name is Elisha."

"Yes, ma'am," Finnegan said. "Much obliged."

An awkward silence of brief duration ensued; then Glazer said, "Well, now that the formalities have been taken care of, I suggest we eat before everything gets cold."

Harbaugh assisted Elisha with her chair then quickly claimed the seat next to her. Finnegan hesitated before taking a place between Butler and Brunston. Glazer said grace, and then the cook and his helper came in from the kitchen and began serving. During the main course, except for courteous exchange, the diners ate heartily.

Afterwards, Brunston said, "Your speech sounds like you're from down the river, Clint."

"Yes sir, New Orleans."

"I haven't made it there as yet," Major Brunston said. "But I certainly plan to some day. Real pretty country, I hear."

"About as pretty as it gets," Finnegan replied. "But the heat and the bugs can be a problem."

"Let me say amen to that, friend," Butler the businessman said with a shake of his head. "I spent some time there working the bayous for hides. The mosquitoes about drove me out of my mind."

"Did you serve in the war, Mr. Finnegan?" Harbaugh questioned, his manner intent.

"Yes."

"With the Confederates, I suppose?"

"That's right."

"Clint rode with Colonel Mosby," Glazer explained.

"An enlisted man, were you?" Harbaugh persisted.

"Initially. But after six months I was commissioned a lieutenant. And a year later I was promoted to captain."

"Might you have been at Bull Run?" Major Brunston inquired. "Or should I say Manassas?"

"Guess it doesn't matter much. I missed the first battle but made the second."

"The same with me," Brunston said. "Can't tell you how happy I was to get out of there in one piece. You folks were downright inhospitable."

"Well, as I recall, the Union wasn't all that neighborly either," Finnegan countered.

"Let's just be thankful we made it through," Brunston said. "Many of our brothers didn't fare as well."

"True enough." Finnegan looked to Butler. "What kind of hides were you after in the bayous?"

"Gators mostly, along with some copperheads and moccasin. We also took what river otters were available, though the occasion was rare."

"You a trapper?"

"I was once. But I'm a trader now. Me and Winthrup here are headed for the Dakota Territory. We're looking to do some business in the fur trade. If things work out, we could do all right for ourselves."

"The markets are wide open up there, or so we've been told," said Winthrup.

"A man would want to go real careful above Fort Sully to the head of the Yellowstone," Brunston interjected. "Been quite a few reports of Sioux war parties around there lately. They don't have much love for the white man these days."

Winthrup considered the major's words with a furrowed brow. "I was told the army was keeping them calmed down."

Responding sarcastically, Brunston said, "That's what a lot of folks in Washington are preaching. But there's not a wit of truth to it. We simply don't have the troops to get the job done. I take it this is your first trip to the territory?"

"Uh, well, yes it is," Winthrup conceded with obvious reluctance. "But I frankly don't see why the Indians would be all that interested in a couple of traveling businessmen."

"Are you going to the trapping grounds on your own?" Glazer inquired with evident concern.

"That's our plan," Winthrup replied.

"Don't do it," Major Brunston said. "Come sundown of the first day, your hair will be hanging in some brave's tepee. What's more, that fancy stickpin you got there won't be buried with you either."

"Aren't you being a bit dramatic, Major?" protested Elisha.

Brunston offered the young woman a thin smile. "Miss Parkinson, I'm afraid folks from the east have a rather romantic view of what goes on out here."

"You're intimating that all Indians are dangerous, as liable to burn and plunder as not?"

"No, ma'am," said the major. "But you have to understand they have a way of life much different than ours. In many tribes a brave isn't considered to be a man until he's killed someone. Most braves are raised from a pup to be warriors. So when their tribe is threatened, they are trained and skilled at killing their enemy."

"Isn't there an Indian with you?" Butler inquired pointedly.

Brunston nodded. "He's a scout. Been one for several years now. Rode alongside me in all kinds of trouble and doesn't have any family. He saw them killed in a Sioux raid. I trust him implicitly. Many a time he could have taken my hair, or left me to die. But he always risked his own life to save mine."

"What makes him the exception to the rule?" Elisha asked.

"He's a Flathead, a people with a sense of community who usually don't make trouble for their neighbors," Brunston continued. "They're a different tribe. Besides he has shown his loyalty while the Sioux, Cheyenne, and Arapaho have fought tooth and nail to keep whites out and to preserve their way of life."

"He told me his name is Creek," Finnegan said.

"Yes." Major Brunston laughed. "That's because he was born on the bank of a creek. Or so he claims anyway. The Sioux regard him as a traitor. If he was caught, they'd treat him to a real slow and painful death."

Elisha waved her hand in a dismissing fashion. "With all due respect, Major," she said, "I have never heard my father speak of Indians in such a bloodthirsty manner."

Brunston's jaw tightened imperceptibly. "Well now, Miss Parkinson," he said quietly, "once we reach Fort Randall you can learn how things are for yourself. It's about this time of year that the braves go out seeking conquest over who they see as invaders into their territory. They'll attack whatever is handy, even a steamboat."

"Attack a steamboat?" Her delicate features promptly assumed an anxious expression. "Is that so, Captain?"

Glancing up from his plate, Glazer replied, "Yes, ma'am. It's happened to me a few times."

"But we're in the middle of the river," she persisted, "a good distance from the shore on either side."

"Yes, ma'am. But there are bends in the waterway where it narrows down or sandbars force us toward land. But ordinarily you get a couple of days warning before there's trouble."

"Warning? How do you mean warning, Captain?" Harbaugh inquired, leaning forward in his chair.

"The Indians will follow the boat along the shore until there's a place they can ford with their horses. And then they'll try to get aboard."

Lieutenant Harbaugh ventured a furtive glance at Elisha, noting her discomfort, and said, "I don't think that's very likely in our case."

"Never can tell what a warrior will do," said Glazer.

Her face a grim mask, Elisha pushed back from the table and arose. "If you'll excuse me, I'm tired and would like to get some sleep."

There was a scraping of chair legs on the wooden floor as the men hurriedly got to their feet. Elisha said her farewells and left the room. The others seated themselves—except for Harbaugh.

"I think I'll turn in as well," he said, nodding to Brunston. "Good night, Major."

"Good night, Lieutenant."

Harbaugh looked around. "Good evening to you as well, gentlemen."

After the compartment door closed, the remaining members of the group settled back in their chairs.

"I'd say the lieutenant is sweet on the lady," Winthrup noted casually.

"Could be." Major Brunston grinned. "Don't know if she feels the same way, though."

"I'm afraid the discussion upset the young lady," said Finnegan.

"I agree," Glazer declared. "Gentlemen, we've got apple pie for dessert. I'm going to have some. Anyone care to join me?"

As soon as the last of the diners had left and the cook was clearing off the table, Glazer looked to Finnegan and together they headed for the master cabin. There the captain unlocked the door and entered the room. A lamp atop a writing desk provided the only illumination in the room. The walls were bare except for a series of clothes hooks and a shelf supporting a number of books. Boxes of papers along with a wooden footlocker lay neatly arranged on the floor. A bunk and a straight back chair occupied a far corner.

"Now that you've met everybody, what do you think?" Glazer inquired.

Finnegan shook his head. "I'm a bit uneasy about those fellas going to the Dakota Territory."

"Why?"

"I used to hunt hides in the bayous. And I've met a lot of trappers. But Butler and his friend don't seem like the type."

"My reaction exactly," Glazer said. "And the others?"

"Nothing suspicious, so far as I can tell."

Kneeling down, Glazer lifted the lid of the footlocker and rummaged through its contents. As he did, Finnegan stole a glance at a book lying open on the desk. It appeared to be a diary. He looked closer. One of the pages was dated June 14, 1866. His gaze moved to a handwritten paragraph and read, "I believe there to be danger of an armed intervention, and I am taking appropriate precautions." Glazer came to his feet.

"No doubt you're familiar with these," he said, producing two cap and ball pistols. "They're just like the one I'm wearing."

"Yes sir," Finnegan said. "I've used an Army Colt like those any number of times."

Finnegan took one of the pistols and felt its weight. It balanced nicely.

"Are you armed?" asked the captain.

"No, I didn't have a chance to replace the one I left with a friend. I see now that was an error in judgment."

"Take this one and I'll give you a shoulder holster to go with it. But, mind you, it'll have to come out of your pay."

"Thank you, sir."

"In the trunk I keep a supply of extra powder, caps, and ammunition." Glazer said. "And I've got something else I want to show you."

He knelt, returned one of the pistols to the chest, and closed the lid. Swinging around, he withdrew a large canvas sheath from under the bed. Untying a cord, he pulled back a flap to reveal the butt of a rifle.

"It's the very latest thing—a new 1866 Winchester carbine equipped with lever action."

Finnegan squinted at it in an appraising manner. "Designed a lot like the old Henry Repeater."

"Pretty much the same pattern," Glazer said. "At first Winchester was selling it as the Improved Henry, but it shoots the same cartridge—a .44 Henry rimfire. The magazine is for fifteen cartridges, but I put in fourteen, and instead of loading from the top there's a side chamber. See? Check it over."

With practiced ease Finnegan clamped the butt of the stock against his shoulder and sighted down the barrel. He squeezed off a round in his mind's eye, then worked the leaver action, utilizing the last three fingers of his right hand. The metal lever swung to and fro in well-oiled action.

"A beauty, don't you think?" Glazer said.

"Yes sir. She's that, alright."

"It's one of the few I know of, west of the Mississippi," Glazer explained. "An army friend of mine got it directly from the Winchester Company in New Haven, Connecticut. It's the only one I could get my hands on."

"Too bad you don't have more," said Finnegan.

He pointed at the boxes. "Those papers on top are just for cover. I have enough rifle ammunition in there to start a war. Also, outside my cabin is a small room I use for my armory. Ammunition and fifteen Springfields are stored there. Some of the crew are armed and some aren't. It's what they feel comfortable with. I've also asked the company to get me a cannon for the bow; but no luck this trip."

"You must feel quite strongly that someone is after the army payroll," Finnegan said.

"I'd bet anything on it," Glazer replied. "As I mentioned earlier, I don't believe Scower is here by accident. He could be working with Butler and Winthrup, or he might well be part of something bigger. I don't know. Only we can't afford to be caught napping. That's why I'm showing you these weapons and where they're being kept."

"I see."

Glazer opened a desk drawer and removed a key. "This is to the cabin door and the armory. Use it in case of an emergency."

"I understand."

"Don't let anyone know you've got it. And I mean no one."

"Yes sir."

"Oh, and that reminds me," Glazer continued. "We're going to make an unscheduled stop at Fort Leavenworth. Miss Parkinson wants to telegraph Fort Randall. It seems her father doesn't know she's on her way there for a visit. From what I can gather, she's supposed to be at school in Philadelphia."

Finnegan grinned. "Sounds as though the young lady has a mind of her own."

"Very definitely. I hope she doesn't make trouble for us."

"Didn't Major Brunston refer to her father as 'colonel'?"

"Yes. Colonel Armbruster Parkinson, to be exact. He's been assigned special liaison to Commanding Officer Major Hiram Dryer at Fort Randall. During the war he served under General Tecumseh Sherman. Now his job is to help old 'Bloody Bill' solve the Indian problem."

His face hardening, Finnegan said, "If he served with General Sherman, then killing and burning shouldn't hold any hesitation for him."

A quick glance convinced Glazer that it would be best to let the subject die.

"The map I want you to study is over there," he said, motioning toward a leather packet lying on the bunk. "Remember now—I need you to know our course backwards and forwards as soon as possible. Perhaps you'd better study it in the dining room. Don't let me down."

"I won't, sir."

When Finnegan carrying the map case reached the door, he felt a hand on his arm.

"Do you recall how I spoke about our mutual trust when you hired on?" Glazer said.

"Yes sir."

"I kind of went behind your back the day we left port."

Finnegan frowned. "How so?"

"That morning, I checked with some of my friends at army headquarters in St. Louis. I was able to verify that you did indeed serve with Colonel

Mosby. A few of the officers there knew about you from the war. One of them even claimed to have been a captive of yours briefly after a fight at a saw mill on the eve of Second Manassas."

Finnegan nodded. "I recall the incident, but not the officer."

"He spoke of how solicitously you treated the Union wounded."

"It was no different than I would have expected if the situation had been the other way around."

"Nevertheless, I felt much more secure about placing my confidence in you. And it's for this reason that I brought you to my cabin tonight. Without your assistance, I'm a man alone."

"Rest assured, Captain, we're in this together. I'm not forgetting that you saved my life, sir."

Glazer seemed to take heart.

"Scower's in the wheelhouse now," he said, "and I'm going to relieve him. It's best that he doesn't see that I gave you the map."

"Yes sir."

When Finnegan was gone, Glazer drew out his pistol and went over to the desk. In the light of the lamp he spun the gun's cap and ball cylinder and checked each chamber. There was no other choice but to trust his new assistant master. He smiled to himself. *A Yankee and a Reb. Now isn't that ironic.*

CHAPTER FOUR

As far as the eye could see, the land was transitioning into early summer. Greenery was everywhere—the trees were spreading their leaves along the river and where the rains had pooled, thick grass lay in the depressions and hollows. Wavering growth spread across the gently heaving plains bordering the river. Overall, the vast expanse spread unendingly toward the horizon with the only real hindrance being a cluster of trees at the water's edge. Their leafy branches formed a network of green across the blue palate of an inviting sky. Kansas lay to the starboard of the course that the Dakota Dawn so resolutely traversed. A tempestuous current occasionally swirled around the vessel, slowing the ship, and the great expanse of Missouri formed the shoreline to the port side.

Finnegan and Master Glazer peered through the windows of the wheelhouse at a cluster of buildings now coming into view.

"Fort Leavenworth?" Finnegan questioned, indicating the direction.

"That's it," the captain replied. "I'll let you take her to port."

"You sure?"

"Uh-huh. This is as good a spot as any to try your hand."

Although excited about the prospect of performing his inaugural docking, Finnegan did not experience the nervousness which previously accompanied such first-time situations. Since departing St. Louis, he had spent a good number of hours handling the huge steamer under a variety of conditions. Now the docking required him to counter the perverse ebb and flow of the river. Steering was almost second nature to him. Reflexively, Finnegan began to nudge the prow of the boat toward the fast-closing bank even while gauging the resistance of the water as transmitted to his hands through the helm.

"Turn the wheel—easy as you go," Glazer said. "Blow the whistle to throttle down the engine."

Finnegan pulled the cord suspended overhead and the steam whistle on the roof of the wheelhouse gave vent to a deafening blast. Twice more he signaled. Within moments the boat began to lose momentum as the safety locks atop the firebox opened, allowing heat to escape into the air instead of the boilers. As a result the connecting rods from the engine lost their power and the paddlewheel gradually ceased its churning.

"Let the bow come back about two degrees until the stern gets in line and watch out for that docked steamboat," Glazer instructed. "All right now—gently let the drift take us in parallel to the shore."

With something of a sidling action the Dakota Dawn slipped toward the bank until one of the crew members jumped over the side and secured the hawser line. Even as the boilers shut down, a wooden ramp was bridging the gap between the main deck and the pier. The other steamboat was docked to port.

"Good job, Mister Clint Finnegan. Very good job. You are indeed a quick learner."

"Thank you, sir."

Finnegan tethered the wheel in place and followed Glazer to the cabin area. There Elisha and Harbaugh waited.

"I ask that you dispatch your business as quickly as possible, ma'am," Glazer said. "The river makes schedules difficult enough to keep without undue delays."

Elisha smiled. "I won't abuse your courtesy, Captain."

When they were ashore, Glazer laid a hand on Finnegan's shoulder.

"Tell the men they're at liberty to visit the fort store but there's not to be any drinking. I'll sound the whistle when it's time to get underway."

"Yes sir."

"If you lack anything, better see to it now," Glazer advised.

"Do you need an advance?"

"No sir. I kept something back from the bank."

Glazer nodded and started for his cabin, then hesitated. "Be careful," he said in a subdued tone, "and don't utter a word about the payroll."

"Not to worry, sir."

Finnegan carried out the shipmaster's orders. Then he walked with Duke to the head of the ramp and surveyed the fort. It was a colorless sprawl of long, low buildings spaced inside a large enclosure.

The vista around it was unobstructed for miles making the possibility of a surprise attack patently impossible. Without a doubt the army had intended the installation to be a permanent one.

"Come on, boy. Let's stretch our legs a bit."

He affectionately roughed the dog behind the ears then glanced over his shoulder. In a nearby cargo compartment Creek sat cross-legged beside the horses, arms folded and head bowed as though in deep reflection. His very posture defied interruption.

Once ashore, Finnegan paused to consider the other steamboat. It was of side-wheel construction named "Western Sun" and easily matched the Dakota Dawn in size. Stacks of wood stood beside the fire box while aft the hold contained row upon row of kegs and barrels. Everywhere men labored with the unloading process.

"You from the Dakota Dawn?"

The voice's authoritative tone jarred Finnegan out of his reverie.

"Uh, yes…sir."

A stooped, heavily bearded man wearing a captain's cap and coat had posed the question.

"Is Master Glazer aboard?" the man inquired.

"Yes sir. He should be in his cabin."

"Much obliged."

The man set out for the Dakota Dawn at a brisk pace.

Reaching the compound, Finnegan studied the flow of faces that passed him on either side. There were a few smiles now and again, but most of the expressions seemed determined in nature, denoting a singleness of purpose. And the soldiers on duty at the main gate were armed and very attentive to the comings and goings. Inside the complex recruits drilled on an open field while horses and wagons seemed to be everywhere.

At length Finnegan espied a sign identifying a weathered building as a general store. He made for it, only to be distracted by the sight of a crowd gathering several yards beyond. Curious, he went to see what was attracting so many people. Through a gap between the heads of those standing to the front he saw Scower belligerently confronting Mase Woodson, the big black man who tended the boilers on the Dakota Dawn. From the front line of onlookers the deckhand Watts emerged and took Woodson's arm as if to lead him away. But Scower shoved Watts and sent him sprawling onto the damp turf. The crowd roared its approval. Watts rose slowly and Scower promptly went after him. Woodson stepped forward, a placating smile on his lips.

"Fighting ain't the way, Mr. Scower," he said. "You're stowing too much anger. The devil's got a grip on your soul. Best shed him before he takes you down to the pit."

Scower cursed and drew back to smash the smiling face. It was then Finnegan caught his arm and cuffed him hard across the mouth. The sound was like the crack of a whip. Now the crowd which had been clamoring for him, grew silent. Blood trickled from Scower's split lips. He swiped at them with the back of his hand, eyes glowering hatefully.

"I'm gonna kill you," he rasped.

Without a word Finnegan hit him again. Scower's head snapped back and he half turned in his tracks.

"No need to go fighting over old Mase," Woodson said, extending a hand to restrain the two men.

Watts, with gentle words and a persistent grip, drew Woodson off through the ring of spectators whose attention was riveted upon the two adversaries in their midst.

Recovering quickly, Scower plowed into Finnegan, shoulders bulled and powerful legs driving. They went down together in a tangle of flailing arms. Scower finished sitting on top of Finnegan. He tried gouging, but Finnegan caught an errant finger between his teeth and bit down hard. Howling with pain, Scower halted his assault. Then a forearm across the throat bent Will Scower backward and he tumbled off his seat and to the ground gasping for breath. Finnegan scrambled to his feet, poised for the attack he knew would come.

With effort, Scower rose and ejected a clot of blood-laced sputum. He closed in again, only this time utilizing caution. They sparred briefly before Scower half lunged, sending a meaty fist on a vicious arc aimed for the side of Finnegan's head. But it just encountered air. Scower teetered off balance when something exploded in his ribs, sending a rush of pain through him. Dazed, he wobbled uncertainly. Even as he attempted to steady himself, rock-hard knuckles thudded against his jaw. The ground jumped up to meet him with bone-rattling force.

Still, the cultivated instinct of a barge fighter would not let Scower rest. Deep within the fog-shrouded reaches of his brain came remembrance of a knife, the one he had concealed in his boot for use in an emergency. Rough fingers freed the blade from its makeshift scabbard just as a shower of cold water wrenched him back to full clarity of mind. Strength welled anew within him, spawned by an overwhelming desire to destroy his tormentor.

Finnegan threw the man aside who had tossed the bucket of water. But he could have no more thought for him now. Scower was coming again, this time clutching a knife. Anger filled Finnegan, searing his better judgment. He hadn't wanted trouble—only to be left alone to pursue a new life on the river. But this Scower, this backwater pug, figured to carve his dream to pieces. Well, that wasn't going to happen. Not if he could help it. And he definitely could.

To Scower's surprise, Finnegan came right for him. Was he going to just walk into the blade? No, it had to be some sort of trick. But what? Scower hesitated, remaining in a half crouch. A confused expression commanded his battered features. Finnegan bore in, fists at the ready. He feinted with one hand and Scower put out an arm to parry the expected blow. Scower's forearm functioned as a blind for the knife which was thrust under it. Finnegan had seen this tactic employed on the New Orleans docks and reacted quickly by stepping back. The blade slid harmlessly past. Then he kicked Scower full in the chest. Scower bent double, letting the knife slip from his grasp. A slamming fist under the chin stood him erect and then a crushing left hook spread him out on the sod.

Pandemonium broke out all around. A few of the onlookers struggled with one another while others sought to flee the scene. A number of soldiers forged into the center of the grand melee, shouting and swinging clubs. While Finnegan could only stare in disbelief, rough hands were immobilizing his arms.

"You're under arrest, mister," said a captain.

Finnegan frowned. "What...what for?" he stammered.

"Inciting a riot," came the sharp response. "And possibly attempted murder from the looks of that fella on the ground over there."

A contingent of soldiers lifted Scower's body into a waiting wagon.

Finnegan slowly shook his head. This was not a day of which he could be proud.

Duke trotted ahead of them. He paused intermittently to look back, making certain the man creatures were following.

CHAPTER FIVE

"I'm much in your debt, Captain," Finnegan said breaking the silence which had prevailed between them since they left the hearing room. "That colonel had every intention of bringing me up on charges."

Glazer nodded. "And he would have done it too."

They passed through the main gate of the compound and then turned toward the river where the Dakota Dawn was moored. Once beyond the hearing of the sentries, Glazer said, "I'm also indebted to you, in a manner of speaking."

Finnegan regarded him quizzically. "How's that, Captain?"

"Well, you got Scower out of my hair. He's going to be in the hospital for a good while. On the other hand, I'm now shy of an experienced man at the wheel with the most treacherous stretch of the river still in front of us."

He paused gazing into the distance. "So I'll have to count on you not making a liar out of me."

"A liar, sir?"

"Yes, I told the colonel I desperately needed you in the wheelhouse. Without you, we couldn't deliver the payroll to the Cow Island garrison. I said you were a match of any steersman on the Missouri or the Mississippi."

Finnegan reacted in an explosion of breath. "Lord have mercy!"

"Then I showed the colonel the depositions from Woodson and Watts."

"What depositions?"

Glazer smiled. "They testified that as assistant master, you were acting to prevent any strife among the crew of the Dakota Dawn. And because of Scower's hostile behavior you had no choice but to defend yourself."

"I was under the impression Watts and Woodson can neither read nor write," Finnegan stated.

"They can't," Glazer replied. "I wrote up their statements, then read everything to them."

"Who did the signing, you?"

"I did. A couple of Xs on a document as a legal and binding deposition just wouldn't pass muster."

"No, sir, I shouldn't think so."

"There was nothing illegal or improper done."

"Yes sir."

More silence. Then Glazer said, "A man with a prison record isn't likely to be considered for a pilot's license...ever."

Finnegan nervously cleared his throat. "I certainly appreciate what you did for me today. And I apologize for the trouble. But given the same circumstances, I don't know of anything that might have been done differently. Scower was going to embarrass and hit Mase Woodson, knowing he wouldn't fight back, and he was also beating on Benjamin Watts."

"I understand," Glazer said. "Watts told me the whole story."

Dusk was descending when they reached the river bank and the Dakota Dawn already had its running lights lit.

"Clint," Glazer said pointedly. "You've got to be the steersman Scower was and more. We have to deliver that army payroll along with the rest of the cargo safely and on time or I'm mud. And so are you. For a fact, we're flush up against it."

Finnegan nodded. "I know that map backward and forward. And you said I have a natural touch for the wheel. Things will work out. You'll see."

"I hope so." Glazer enunciated the words softly, wistfully. "I sure hope so."

They went aboard, each man captive to his own thoughts.

CHAPTER SIX

Pieces of trees and debris, lodged in the mud, were appearing much more frequently now. It was an indication that the spring run-off was lessening. And whenever a pilot saw these signs he experienced a sense of anxiety, even dread. Large masses of earth, wood and stone buried in the river could tear a hole in the hull of a steamer and sink it within minutes.

Given these thoughts, Finnegan found himself gripping the wheel with knuckle-whitening tension. He exhaled forcibly and relaxed his hands.

"Mind if I join you?" said a soft voice.

Looking around, Finnegan was surprised to see Elisha standing in the wheelhouse doorway. He hesitated before responding, "No, ma'am, but I don't think Captain Glazer would approve."

"I won't get in the way," she said entering. "I promise."

The heady scent of perfume accompanied her. It filled his nostrils and stirred his pulse. She stood off to one side.

"You were very fortunate back there at the fort," she said.

He glanced over to see her staring at him, the hint of a smile on her lips. She wore a print dress of simple design which exposed her neck and gathered in pleated fashion at the waist. Without all the glitter, she seemed younger; more a girl than a woman of the world. It definitely was an impression he much preferred.

"I've been on enough army posts to know that you could have gotten up to six months hard labor," she continued.

"Do you suppose that's what Colonel Armbruster Parkinson would have given me?" he inquired evenly.

"He could have; what's your point?" There was a note of challenge to her voice.

"I understand the colonel served with General Sherman during his campaign through Georgia," Finnegan replied, his eyes fixed on the river. "Being a party to all that, I shouldn't think he would have given too much thought concerning some southern fella caught fighting."

Elisha was quiet for a time. He could have kicked himself for expressing to her his anger over the war. It was stupid to say such a thing. It just slipped out.

"What do you know about General Sherman?" she asked.

"Only what I've been told by folks who survived the burning and killing."

"Many of the general's officers, my father included, believed him to be insane," she said. "Early in his career he suffered a nervous breakdown that forced him to leave the army. When he returned there was a noticeable change in his personality. He spoke of war as a process of extermination, a means of ridding oneself of its enemies."

"Is that what he plans for the Indians?"

"Yes. Yes, I'm sure of it."

Another glance found her gazing vacantly at the passing landscape.

"Worried about your father?"

She nodded, tears brimming in her eyes.

"That's what I thought," he said. "Especially after the way you crossed swords with Major Brunston the other night."

He took a bandanna from a shirt pocket and held it out.

"Thank you." She dabbed at her damp face.

A powerful urge to take her in his arms, to comfort her, possessed him. It was all he could do to resist the temptation.

"I'm very fearful there's going to be an Indian war." She returned the bandanna. "I've heard it said in Philadelphia and Washington. More senseless fighting and dying on both sides."

"You knew this and came ahead anyway?"

"Oh, yes," she replied. "You see, he's the only family I have now. Mother died late last year. After this special assignment my father planned to retire. Then we were going to live in Connecticut, near Hartford. We have a house there."

"You must love your father very much."

"Yes, I do. You see, when I learned my father would be involved with what they call the 'Indian control problem', the only thing that mattered to me was my being with him. I didn't want him left alone, not again. If war breaks out I want to be close at hand. I know Father would never approve my coming, so I came anyway."

Before Finnegan could reply she was at the wheelhouse door and had opened it.

"I know why you were fighting at Fort Leavenworth," she said. "You did a very noble thing. And for what it's worth, I feel quite sure my father would have let you off, too."

She turned and was gone. *Why did she come to visit?* he asked himself. *Bored? Lonely? Just wanted to pass the time of day? In any event she could have talked with Lieutenant Harbaugh. He was always hovering around her like a bee to honey. No, she must have had a very good reason for coming up to the wheelhouse. Could it be she simply wanted to see me?* He smiled at the thought.

CHAPTER SEVEN

Many days had gone by since the Dakota Dawn left port at St. Louis. Time passed quickly when you were guiding a nearly four-hundred ton steamboat up one of the most treacherous rivers known to man. Each day he gained more confidence in his ability. And so did Captain Glazer.

It was just before sunrise and the glow of the running lights reflected brightly off the calm, dark waters. It felt as though the boat was gliding on a cushion of air. Both boilers were functioning at less than a third of capacity which reduced the need for more cautious steering. Finnegan's primary concern under these conditions was to be on the lookout for oncoming vessels along with snags and other dangerous obstructions. In moments like this, he could safely keep watch while still entertaining his thoughts in relative peace and quiet. For this reason he didn't mind working the early morning turn at the helm.

Stifling a yawn, Finnegan let the wheel turn back easily with the run of the current. Nebraska City lay hours behind and Omaha and Council Bluffs landings were due just after dawn. Then there would follow a long stretch before the Missouri River veered west above Sioux City. Although he had never been this way before, the route was clear in his mind, as depicted on Glazer's maps. So distracted was he with a variety of loosely related considerations that the muffled thumping sound forward failed to attract his full attention. But he became starkly alert when a light could be seen bobbing off the starboard bow. With one hand he raised the wheelhouse window on that side and heard the faint exchange of voices. Had someone come aboard? Should he secure the wheel and investigate or blow the steam whistle?

Even as Finnegan pondered a course of action, Major Brunston was below in his cabin busily initiating a carefully contrived plan. A half hour before he had broken into the armory and secreted the Springfield rifles to the main deck. Fully dressed, he took a final look at the large strong box containing the army payroll, then went to the cabin door and quietly opened it. He surveyed the adjoining hallway. As ordered, an enlisted man slumbered there. The major approached and with a firm hand shook the man's shoulder.

"Uh? What ...oh," the soldier mumbled, his heavy-lidded eyes gazing dumbly into the major's face.

Brunston put a finger to his lips and said, "Come with me, Sergeant."

"Yes sir."

Returning to his cabin, Brunston motioned toward the strong box on the bunk bed.

"I'll need you to carry that to the deck, Sergeant," he said.

When the young man moved to the bunk he was struck on the back of the head with the butt of a service revolver. He sagged without a sound and was lowered to the floor. Brunston slipped a knife from his pocket and began cutting up the bed sheet. The strips were used to bind the sergeant hand and foot. And then a handkerchief was stuffed into his mouth as a gag.

Once again Brunston entered the hall and took a careful look around before proceeding to a cabin down the way and knocking lightly. The door swung back to reveal Winthrup holding a gun on Butler.

"Guess this is where we dissolve our partnership, friend," Winthrup said grinning.

Butler made no reply, his face devoid of expression. The three men walked towards the dining room.

"Sit him over there," Brunston whispered indicating a far corner. "I'll roust the others."

Winthrup escorted Butler to the designated chair while Major Brunston went to Harbaugh's cabin and knocked. Within a few moments there was a stirring from within. The latch slipped and the door opened. Harbaugh regarded his superior with a questioning frown. Only belatedly did he realize that the business end of a Colt .36 was pressed against his belly.

"Just come out easy, Lieutenant," Brunston said, "and join the party."

On the way out of the room, the major picked up the lieutenant's belt, pistol, and holster. Lieutenant Harbaugh was guided to the dining room. Then Major Brunston captured Captain Glazer in a similar manner and he also came under the guard of Alonzo Winthrup in the dining room.

Concerned about the sounds that came to him from the raised window, Finnegan tied down the wheel and hurried to the compartment door. When he reached the cabin deck a man stepped out of the dark to confront him, a shotgun at the ready.

"Hold it right there and grab some sky," the man said.

Finnegan considered the double barrels pointed at his chest, and complied. A gloved hand removed a pistol from Finnegan's belt.

"All right, let's go down to the water line," the man said, moving to one side.

Even in the poor light Finnegan could discern that his captor had a handkerchief over his face.

Upon reaching the main deck Finnegan felt the shotgun nudge him in the direction of the bow. He grudgingly acquiesced while trying to make sense of what was taking place. As he drew near the boilers a keelboat could be seen drifting alongside. He noticed Brunston standing beside a thoroughly frightened Elisha.

"Morning, Clint," Major Brunston said affably.

Finnegan nodded, looking at the girl.

"I guess you can figure out what's happening here?" Brunston continued.

"I can."

"Just as you surmised, we're making off with the payroll."

"What's Miss Parkinson got to do with that?"

Brunston smiled. "Why, she's going along so nobody will try and stop us. But before we leave I'll have to ask you a favor."

"Such as?"

"Let me show you." Brunston took a pistol from the holster at his hip and motioned to the man with the shotgun. "Keep the lady company. My friend and I have a little business to transact."

"Right," the man replied.

"After you, Clint." Brunston gestured toward the stern of the boat.

They walked single file in silence while approaching the cargo hold where yet another masked man armed with a rifle kept the entire crew confined.

"We'll be leaving shortly; we'll load the rifles then." Brunston told the man in passing. "There's only one more thing that has to be done."

"Yes sir."

"To the fuel bin," Brunston ordered, "Second thought, wait a minute." He pointed toward an ax leaning against a pile of corded wood. "Now that should do nicely. Get it."

When Finnegan hesitated, Brunston said, "Now...before I lose my patience." There was a no-nonsense tone to his voice. "And don't think about trying anything."

Finnegan appropriated the ax and Brunston said, "Now to the engine compartment. Just do as I tell you and everything will be fine. Understand?"

Finnegan nodded his head.

The engine room emitted a subdued hissing sound, receiving just enough steam power to turn the paddlewheel.

"Which of these controls the rudder?" Brunston singled out a pair of wooden struts attached to a descending metal rod.

"Both of them," Finnegan responded. "They're called tiller arms."

"How interesting," Brunston grinned. "Now, you take that ax and smash them both."

Eyes widening in surprise, Finnegan said, "If I do that we won't be able to steer the boat."

"Uh-huh." The barrel of the pistol raised in menacing fashion. "Now lay to it."

With an air of sullen resignation Finnegan swung the ax in powerful measured strokes that drove the sharply beveled edge of the ax deep into the wood. In a matter of minutes the tiller arms were completely severed from their connections.

"Nice. Very nice," Brunston said. "Now that leaves just those metal rods which turn the paddlewheel. Give them a couple of good licks, too."

Finnegan turned the ax over and used the flat part of the head like a hammer. Each blow gave a ringing sound as the rods gradually relented, first bending, and finally breaking off their connection.

"Captain Glazer is going to be madder than a wet hen when he finds out what's been done to his precious boat," Brunston said, grinning again. "But we can't have him contacting the army until we get clear of here. No, sir, we can't allow that to happen."

Wearily Finnegan ran a sleeve over his dripping face. He was trying to buy time, trying to figure out some means of preventing the robbery. Could he possibly throw the...?

"Now drop that ax right there," Brunston said as though reading his mind. "Go on, do it."

The ax fell to the floor.

"Let's get out of here," directed Brunston, motioning with the pistol barrel.

Out on the main deck Brunston called to a gunman standing guard over the crew.

"When we get to the front of the boat, I'll give a whistle," he said. "Bring that bundle of rifles and come running."

"Yes, boss."

At the foot of the steps to the cabin deck, Finnegan felt a restraining hand on his shoulder.

"Up you go," Brunston ordered. "And do so carefully. I really don't want to shoot you at this late stage."

Finnegan climbed the steps then waited on Brunston.

"All right, let's visit your friends."

Inside the dining area they found Butler, Harbaugh, and Glazer standing in a corner under Winthrup's gun.

"Looks like we're ready to take our leave," Brunston said, motioning for Finnegan to join the others.

Winthrup rose from his chair. "They've been downright docile," he noted. "Peaceful as lambs."

Glazer glared at his tormentor but kept silent.

Not so Harbaugh. His features pinched in an expression of anger and he said, "Major, you're ruining your career. I beg you to reconsider what you're doing."

"Man can't live on pride," Brunston said. "I just look at it as taking early retirement."

"How are you going to explain kidnapping?" Butler demanded.

"We aren't kidnapping anybody," Winthrup replied. "The young lady simply accepted our invitation to take a little trip."

"At the point of a gun?" Butler challenged. "Some invitation."

"Enough talk," shouted Brunston. "Alonzo, you get below and I'll be along directly."

Winthrup nodded and left.

"Captain Glazer, as Finnegan here will tell you, I found it necessary to stall your boat."

"What's that supposed to mean?" demanded Glazer.

"Explain it to him, Clint."

"Captain," Finnegan began, "the major had me take an ax to the tiller arms and the connecting rods. So as things stand we can neither steer nor turn the paddlewheel."

Glazer paled noticeably and the veins of his neck bulged. He opened his mouth to speak, hesitated, and then remained silent.

"If Clint hadn't done it, I would have shot him," Brunston said. "Should anybody try to follow us, we'll kill the girl."

"Where do you figure to hide, Major?" Butler asked.

Brunston chuckled. "There's a lot of country out in the territories."

"What...what are you going to do with Miss Parkinson?" Lieutenant Harbaugh questioned.

"If she cooperates and nobody gives us any trouble, we'll send her along to Fort Randall." Brunston retreated to the doorway. "So long, gentlemen. Nice knowing you."

Brunston closed the door and they heard something being jammed against it. Finnegan tried it and it wouldn't budge.

The captain jumped up and rushed into the adjoining galley. Once there he took a key from his pocket and unlocked the door to the hall. Running hard, he reached his cabin and let himself inside. He threw back the lid of the footlocker and extracted the six-shooter.

"Don't do it, Captain," Finnegan warned lunging into the room. "You might hit the girl."

Without responding, Glazer smashed a cabin window and thrust his arm through the opening. He aimed carefully at the silhouette of a man on the keelboat and fired. Immediately there were return shots which further shattered the glass and he ducked for cover.

"It's too late, Captain. If you shoot that girl, you'll never forgive yourself."

Continuing to ignore Finnegan, Glazer scrambled under the bunk and pulled out the Winchester repeater. Once again he went to the window and Finnegan grabbed the rifle and tore it from Glazer's hands.

"Not too smart, Captain," Butler said from the doorway. "Your chance of stopping them is next to nil. Odds are you alerted every Indian within hearing distance."

Glazer slumped onto the bunk and sat there in morose anger.

CHAPTER EIGHT

The current swept the boat aimlessly downstream. Glazer and several members of the crew remained in the engine room trying to repair the damage. But it proved to be a hopeless task. The captain returned to the deck just as light was breaking on the distant horizon.

"I'm sorry, Captain," Finnegan said.

"Sorry doesn't change anything," said Glazer. "We've got to save the boat."

"Captain, I'll do anything you ask."

Just then Butler appeared.

"I think it's time I put my cards on the table, gentlemen," Butler said taking a badge from inside his coat. "I'm a federal marshal assigned to protect the army payroll. Unfortunately, I didn't do a very good job."

"Blast it!" exclaimed Glazer. "We've got a boat to save and we can talk later."

Just then crewman Watts came forward. "Captain we're about to ram the shore," he announced.

Watts ran to the bow and pointed to the west bank. Captain Glazer, Finnegan, and Butler followed. Downstream and dead ahead, a little more than a hundred yards, a segment of the shoreline jutted abruptly into the river.

"Put every man on a pole," Glazer commanded. "We aren't drifting that fast. Maybe we can prevent the hull from being caved in, or worse."

"Aye, Captain," said Watts.

"All hands stand by for collision!" shouted Glazer. "Man your poles!"

The deckhands rushed to comply. Glazer turned to Finnegan.

"Take the lead position, Clint," he said. "You've done this kind of thing on a flatboat. Show the others what to do."

"Yes sir," said Finnegan grabbing a pole.

Clint moved to the bow, all the while studying the projection of land which was steadily approaching on a collision course. Its bank consisted of a low, narrow shelf of mud rising at a sharp angle from the water. Further shoreward, there was a mix of tree roots and rocks. His gaze swept the river for any telltale ripples or eddies which would indicate the presence of an obstruction beneath the surface. Nothing caught his eye. But he could be mistaken.

When the boat was twenty-five yards from the point, he lowered the tip of the pole into the water and met no resistance. This indicated that the wash along the river was deep and so far did not offer them a chance to maneuver. Squatting he thrust the pole in the water and once again failed to make contact. A third time his pole encountered sand.

"All right, poles in!" he shouted over his shoulder. "Strong push off the bow and starboard!"

Short, powerful probes from the bow and a gradual leveraging action at the starboard side produced a yawing motion. The Dakota Dawn was slowing and angling towards the western shore.

"Everybody to starboard and push!" Finnegan commanded.

With the poles pushing against the river bottom on the starboard side, the steamboat gradually coasted near the muddy outcropping. The natural drift of the current aligned the boat parallel to the shore and she shifted against the mud embankment. Gently the Dakota Dawn dragged herself against the soft bottom and slowly came to a halt. A destructive crash had been averted.

"Tie up fore and aft!" Glazer ordered. "Good job, men! Lady Luck was on our side. We couldn't do that again if we tried."

Immediately several crew members shouldered hawser ropes and climbed overboard. When the lines were secured to trees, Finnegan briefly surveyed the situation then took the stairs to the upper deck. Glazer and Butler met him at the entrance to the dining room and they went inside.

"You had better put some lookouts on that hill," Butler said. "Should Indians come nosing around, we're going to need all the warning we can get."

Glazer went to the compartment door. "Watts!" he yelled. "Report on the double."

Within moments Watts appeared.

"I want volunteers to serve as sentries," Glazer said. "There could be Indians out there."

"Have to say the very same thought crossed my mind, Captain," Watts replied. "I'm ready. And a number of the other boys will be too. But we're gonna need guns."

Glazer made no response but headed for his cabin. He returned shortly with the Colt Peacemaker and the Winchester rifle.

"I know you're familiar with the pistol," he said, "but...

"No worries, sir." Watts grinned. "Us old Johnny Rebs know which end to use."

"Good," Glazer said. "Then I'll put you in charge of the detail." He handed over the weapons. "They're loaded. And here's a bag with caps, powder and shot, and a couple boxes for the Winchester."

Watts took weapons and bag in hand, saluted smartly, and left.

Glazer turned to Butler. "Now, lawman, what do you have to tell me? You say you're a federal marshal?"

"I am," said Butler.

Glazer glared at the marshal. "Why in the world didn't you identify yourself earlier?"

"I couldn't," Butler replied. "My orders were to operate undercover."

"Did Major Brunston and the other army people know who you were?" Finnegan asked.

"No. I was supposed to engage myself with the passengers and in the process keep an eye on things. My partnership with Alonzo Winthrup was fortunate—or so I thought."

"How did you get hooked up with the likes of Winthrup?" asked Glazer.

"I knew who was going to be aboard and something about each of their backgrounds," Butler explained. "Your company supplied this information to me. I decided to represent myself as a trader and make the acquaintance of Winthrup. The idea was to fit in with the group and better avoid suspicion."

"Did you have any indication that the payroll was in danger of being stolen?" Finnegan asked.

"I thought something might be up when your regular pilot didn't show," Butler responded. "Then Scower conveniently signed on. I found out he had a prison record."

"Really?" Glazer evinced surprise. "With what was he charged?"

"He helped rob a New Orleans shipping company eight years ago. Needless to say, I kept close tabs on him until Finnegan put him in the Leavenworth hospital. After that it became a guessing game and I guessed wrong."

"Just what were you expecting of Scower?" Glazer asked.

"To be one of the holdup men," Butler said. "With him gone I had to quickly find a new suspect. I felt certain the robbers had more than one accomplice on board."

"Can you tell us who was your new suspect?" Finnegan questioned.

Butler grinned sheepishly. "I'm not proud to say, but I thought it was you, Captain."

"Me?" Glazer exploded. "Why that's ridiculous."

"Not really," Butler replied. "You could have arranged to get rid of the regular steamboat pilot. That way Scower could be hired without raising any questions."

"Obviously, you are an extremely poor judge of character," Glazer said with some vehemence.

"No arguing that for this occasion, I'm afraid." Butler shook his head. "I never would have guessed that Major Brunston was the ring leader."

Glazer went to his cabin and returned with a map which he spread across the dining room table.

"I figure we're not far from Portsmouth, and no more than five to ten miles from Omaha and Council Bluffs landings," the captain said pointing out the sites. "We had better send someone on ahead to get help."

"With the Indian activity, that could be a real risky walk," said Butler.

"No need to walk when we can ride," Harbaugh said, approaching from the cabin area. "We have three cavalry ponies down in the cargo hold."

"By thunder, that's right," Glazer said with a snap of his fingers. "Only who will we send?"

"Sergeant Phelps is the best horseman I know," Harbaugh replied. "Let me talk to him."

The lieutenant crossed to Brunston's cabin and leaned inside. Shortly he returned followed by the sergeant, a compactly-built man with a ruddy complexion. His head was wrapped in a bandage.

"Sergeant Phelps claims he's quite able to make the trip," Harbaugh said.

"Think you could stay in the saddle if the Indians were to give you a run?" Butler questioned.

Phelps smiled. "Yes sir. A man can do wonders when he is scared enough."

"Here's what must be done, Sergeant," Glazer said. "You'll have to ride up along this side of the river to Omaha. Just a short ways further north, you'll run into the North Platte and the town of Portsmouth. Stop there first and see if you can get a blacksmith and a carpenter to come to the boat."

"What if he can't get help there?" asked Lieutenant Harbaugh.

"No matter what, the sergeant will have to ford the Platte because I want to send a telegram at Omaha. Certainly he can find help there. All we need is a little carpentry and some metal work."

"And some weapons. Can we be towed up there?" Butler asked.

"That would require a steamer our size or larger," Glazer said. "It's unlikely."

"Where's the nearest telegraph station?" Harbaugh inquired.

"Omaha," Glazer responded. "I'm going to have the sergeant send a message to my office in St. Louis. Tell them what's happened to us and report the theft of the payroll."

"I'm thinking of notifying Colonel Parkinson at Fort Randall that his daughter's been kidnapped?" said Harbaugh.

"Seems to me his command headquarters in St. Louis ought to handle such business," said Captain Glazer."

Butler nodded. "Might be best for all concerned if he received the news through official channels."

"Perhaps so," Harbaugh conceded. "But it definitely ought to be part of the message to St. Louis."

"Absolutely," said the captain.

Glazer went to his cabin for pencil and paper. In his absence Finnegan studied the map, his expression one of deep concentration. After a time he tapped a finger on a thin line extending westward from the Missouri River.

"That's the Platte River," he said. "It's my conviction Major Brunston and his people are traveling in that direction."

"Why would they?" Butler questioned. "That's Indian country. Might as well put a gun to his head."

"Once the telegram is sent, he really can't go south or east with every lawman and the army looking for him," Finnegan replied. "And he certainly wouldn't head north to Fort Randall and points beyond. Besides, he told you there was a whole lot of room to hide in the territories. It stands to reason he thought this out rather thoroughly. Even to the point of having the theft take place near the mouth of the Platte."

"I think Finnegan is right," Lieutenant Harbaugh added. "Major Brunston is not a man to go off half-cocked. Quite to the contrary."

Glazer returned with several sheets of paper and pencil. Harbaugh promptly appropriated them. Then, sitting down, he wrote quickly in a tight, disciplined scrawl.

"Where are you sending that?" Butler asked.

"To the St. Louis command," Harbaugh responded. He finished and handed the note to Sergeant Phelps.

Glazer did the same with his message.

"Gentlemen," said Finnegan. "In studying the map I see the location of Fort Randall is on the Missouri, about two hundred miles northwest from where we're standing. And Fort Kearny is built on the North Platte and is one hundred and seventy miles due west from here."

"What's your point?" asked Lieutenant Harbaugh.

"I'm thinking the major took the girl and the payroll up the Platte. We could follow Brunston from behind and ask the army to cut him off from the north and the west.

"You mean notify Fort Randall and Fort Kearny to send troops?" asked the lieutenant.

"Yes. At least we could try."

Harbaugh's eyes narrowed in a quizzical expression. "We?"

"I was just speaking for myself, actually," said Finnegan.

"You figuring to go after Brunston?" Butler asked.

"Shouldn't somebody?"

The men exchanged glances before Glazer inquired, "Just what do you have in mind, Clint?"

"Creek and I would take the canoe up the Platte in pursuit of the payroll thieves. At the same time an army patrol from Fort Randall and from Fort Kearny could come down and intercept them. Sooner or later Brunston and his people would be trapped."

"What canoe?" Butler asked.

"He's talking about the one I have hanging with the lifeboats," said Captain Glazer. He considered the proposal for a long moment. "You think Brunston will stay on the Platte River…to…where?"

"No telling for certain," Finnegan replied. "He could take it as far as a keelboat can go. But, eventually he has to leave the river and travel by land, if he's heading for California. I'm betting he'll find horses and follow the north fork to the Wyoming Territory. From there he can reach Oregon, Washington, or Canada."

"If he makes it to the Wyoming Territory, chances are there will be no finding him," Butler observed.

"There's another possibility," Finnegan remarked.

"Well, come on, out with it," Glazer said irritably. "Don't just stand there pondering."

"I was going to say Brunston isn't a river man. He's a horse soldier. Besides, I did hear that even a canoe has a hard time going up the Platte because it's so shallow. My bet is that they're meeting someone with horses."

"If they get mounts, what will you do then?" Butler inquired.

"Beg, borrow or steal," Finnegan replied. "I'm counting on Creed to scout for what we need." He read their skepticism and felt a rush of anger. "I know it's a gamble, but I have to try to save that girl."

"There's another factor to be considered as well," Harbaugh stated. "Once Major Brunston and his men feel safe from pursuit, they might just kill Miss Parkinson. I think we should give chase immediately."

"They have half a day's start on us," Finnegan added. "And they won't be able to travel very fast after dark. So we could actually make up time. This, of course, all hinges on what Creek is willing to do. What do you say, Captain?"

"What do the rest of you think?" Glazer asked. "Mr. Butler?"

"If the man's willing to try, then I'm for letting him do it."

"Lieutenant Harbaugh?"

"I approve on one condition. That I go along."

"Fine," said Glazer. He spread his hands in a gesture of resignation and said, "I'm losing my pilot, but my boat's not going anywhere anyway."

"What about weapons?" Butler asked.

Finnegan turned to Glazer. "You'll need your guns to protect the boat."

"I have a service revolver Major Brunston didn't find," Harbaugh said. "When traveling, I always carry an extra one with my personal effects."

Without a word Butler got up and went to his cabin. A few minutes later he returned carrying a belt, holstered pistol and a bag of caps, powder and shot.

"My friend Winthrup was not a very careful fella," said Butler. "He didn't even bother to search my belongings." He handed the items to Finnegan.

Clint secured the buckle so that the revolver rode high on his hip.

"It's a Navy Colt," Butler explained. "I filed off the nose sight so it wouldn't catch on the draw."

"I kind of thought a cavalry man like yourself would be right familiar with a sidearm," said the Marshall. "Now then, there's just one more thing that needs doing."

"What's that?"

"To make this official, I'll deputize you."

Finnegan's eyes widened with surprise. "You're serious?"

"Sure am," Butler replied. "Raise your right hand and repeat after me."

With the completion of the oath, Butler held out a metal star. "As a deputy marshal you're required to have a badge of office handy at all times." he said. "I wouldn't wear it on my shirt. Too good of a target. Most of us wear it concealed."

"I have the ability to arrest Major Brunston?" asked Clint Finnegan.

"You do, if it comes to that."

For several moments Finnegan stared at the object of authority cradled in the palm of his hand.

He had gone from a Confederate rebel to a Yankee lawman. *Well, wonders never cease,* he thought.

Lieutenant Harbaugh retrieved the original message and rewrote it with the new plans and suggestions. Sergeant Phelps tucked the messages inside his jacket then left with Harbaugh at his elbow. Finnegan's gaze followed them down the stairs to the main deck and along the walkway to the cargo hold. He stood beside the wheelhouse and watched the nearby bank. Watts was on land opposite the bow of the boat and another crew member was stationed aft.

Finnegan followed the US Marshall down the stairs to the main deck where Creek stood holding the reins of a saddled mount for Sergeant Phelps.

"Will you go with us after the money and the girl?" he asked the Indian Scout. "Without you there's little hope..."

Creek's face tightened into what might be considered a grin.

"I will go."

"That settles it," said Finnegan. "Captain Glazer, will you look after my dog? He's tied up aft; I'll go tell him to mind his manners."

"Of course," replied Glazer. "All the crew, including me, is partial to that mutt of yours.

Captain Glazer, Marshall Butler, and Harbaugh waited near the bow for Finnegan's return. When he did, Butler approached him.

"God bless you, son." Butler slapped him on the shoulder.

A wooden ramp was laid down between the side of the main deck and the bank. Sergeant Phelps mounted the saddled horse, saluted Lieutenant

Harbaugh, and rode down the ramp onto land. Once assured of solid ground, rider and mount burst forward through the bordering trees and were lost to view. Meanwhile, the canoe was being lowered. When the craft was in the water, Creek, the lieutenant, and Finnegan loaded supplies and climbed aboard. Clint hadn't felt this apprehensive and anxious since the war and the raids with Colonel Mosby.

CHAPTER NINE

Creek squatted in the bow of the canoe smoothly plying the water with his paddle. Finnegan matched him stroke for stroke from his position in the stern. Circumstances were reminiscent of those not long ago days when he canoed the lower Mississippi, eyes peeled for an inviting tributary to explore. Their provisions, wrapped in canvas, were nestled in the bottom of the boat.

Finnegan's mother had never liked the excursions he took up the river. She would watch him go, concern evident in her eyes. A thin, dark-haired woman with a sad smile—that's how he remembered her. Looking back now, he could appreciate the loneliness she must have known with his father gone for days working on a flatboat. Being raised on a Georgia farm where the men folk were always within earshot, she quite naturally didn't take to life as the wife of a man committed to the river. Worse yet was the worry that she could lose her only child to the Big Muddy. Drink finally killed his father. It was more than his mother could bear. When Finnegan became old enough, she went back to her people in Georgia. He remembered her leaving him with a kiss and a teary-eyed backward glance. Odd that he should think about her at a time such as this.

Harbaugh sat in the middle of the boat with Glazer's map spread across his knees. He pointed. "That must be the mouth of the Platte River directly ahead."

Finnegan nodded. Almost in unison he and Creek shifted their paddles to the same side and began pulling hard for the other river. The narrow prow of the boat bit into the current and gradually made its way into the Platte. They found themselves bordered by the broad expanse of Nebraska land.

The sun was a fiery ball. Its brightness lit up the vast plains for miles around. No movement could be discerned in any direction except for a small herd of grazing buffalo. It was an idyllic scene until Creek directed their attention to one disturbing flaw.

"Smoke," he said simply, pointing to a thin spire rising up the river.

"How far?" Finnegan inquired.

"A few miles," came the terse response.

"Indians?"

Creek slowly shook his head. "It's not a signal. Something's burning."

After long minutes of paddling, Harbaugh shaded his eyes against the glare. "It seems to be right on the water line."

"Yes," Finnegan replied. "Kind of odd." He met Harbaugh's searching gaze. "You got that revolver at the ready, Lieutenant?"

"I do."

Squirrels and other creatures along the bank chattered and rustled. Finnegan and Creek dipped their paddles soundlessly in the placid water, barely eliciting a ripple on the surface. As the canoe approached a bend thick with scrub-like vegetation, the smell of burnt wood assailed their nostrils. Paddles withdrawn, they slipped along close to the shoreline using overhanging branches as a means of camouflage. The encroaching shadows clung to their small boat like a great cloak, shielding them from the face of the sun.

Gradually they rounded a roughly-formed finger of land to view the smoldering hulk of a keelboat resting a few yards away. Its bow was pulled up onto the bank and tied to a tree. The fire had gone out and the aft was charred black.

"Major Brunston's?" Harbaugh questioned.

"Could be," Finnegan replied. "Let's get alongside."

Creek brought the canoe flush against the stern of the keelboat. The wood was still warm to the touch.

"Didn't happen that long ago," Harbaugh surmised.

"A few hours at the most," Finnegan said rising carefully. "I'll look around."

He boosted himself over what remained of the keelboat's railing. Then he crouched on the blackened deck. His gaze swept the destruction and settled on a hand. Grasping the appendage, he pulled a body out from debris. The clothing matched one of the robbers. The head was nearly decapitated and the scalp was missing.

Stepping to the side of the deck, Finnegan spoke softly. "There's a dead man up here. I'll see what else I can find."

A feeling of dread filled Clint as he pulled the body further aside to reach a cabin door. It stood ajar. Had they killed the girl? Or taken her with them? He inhaled deeply then slowly let his breath out. Resigned to what must be done, he tried to push aside the door and stumbled over a protruding leg. He grabbed it and yanked. Sweat dripped off his face as he finally managed to disengage the body and pull it onto the open deck. The buckskin leggings were familiar. There were several bloody puncture wounds and the man was also scalped.

Finnegan returned to the cabin and found no other dead. The food supplies, guns and ammunition were gone. Could Brunston, Winthrup, and Elisha have escaped? He hoped Elisha was still alive.

"I found two of the dead robbers and they were both scalped. What now?" Finnegan asked as he lowered himself into the canoe.

"Let's look around on shore," Harbaugh replied. "Creek might be able to come up with something."

The Indian scout sat silently, arms folded across his chest. His face dark and impassive. "I will look for sign," said Creek.

Finnegan picked up his paddle, pushed away from the keelboat, and pulled to a point along the embankment. Foliage provided cover. Creek left the boat and disappeared into the brush. With guns drawn, they sat and waited. In a few moments Creek could be seen coming through the thick growth.

"Come," he whispered. Then he was gone again.

Finnegan and Harbaugh pulled the canoe on shore, then scrambled up the bank and through the brush. Creek crouched under a tree, his gaze fixed on the plain before him.

"Something wrong?" Harbaugh questioned.

"The buffalo are moving."

Peering into the distance, Finnegan said, "I can't see anything. How do you even know there are buffalo out there?"

"I can hear them." Creek put his ear to the ground. "Listen."

For a time Finnegan did the same. "It sounds like faint thunder," he said. "The whole herd is milling around. Do you suppose something is riling them?"

"Yes," Creek replied.

"Wolves, maybe?" Harbaugh asked.

Creek shook his head and pointed to a patch of ground several yards away. "Over there are the prints of horses," he said. "They do not have shoes."

"Indians," Harbaugh remarked.

Finnegan nodded, his thoughts returning to the dead men seen on the keelboat. "How many?"

"Six, maybe seven," Creek responded. "They come with a wagon." He rose and motioned for them to follow. "See, the wheel tracks and the war ponies are together." He indicated the markings in the soft earth. "Wagon horses have shoes."

"Must be a white man," Harbaugh said.

"Or men," Finnegan added.

Even as he spoke, Creek was up and moving toward the tree line. "Two white men and a woman waited here," he said singling out an area of matted grass and crushed earth. "Boot heels make deep marks." A finger prodded some small impressions. "The woman stood with them."

"Brunston, Winthrup, and Elisha," said Finnegan. "So they must be going overland to the territories. That makes our job all the tougher."

"If everybody was on friendly terms then why did the Indians attack the keelboat?" Harbaugh asked.

"They didn't," Creek replied.

"How can you say that?" Finnegan asked. "Both of the dead men were scalped. I saw them."

"There's no sign." Creek led them to the patch of ground once more. "See, none of the war party got off their horses." A sweep of his arm served to demonstrate that there was no evidence of any movement toward the river. He gestured toward the plains. "The wagon and Indians go together."

Harbaugh, his hands clenched into fists, said, "So Brunston and Winthrup must have done the killing. Made it look like the work of Indians."

"To discourage anyone from going after them?" Finnegan asked. "And now they only have to split the payroll money two ways."

"The Major keeps showing me a new side of his character," Harbaugh said. "I have to wonder how a man of his record could do such things."

Turning to Creek, Finnegan asked, "Do you think the Indians are still around?"

Creek nodded. "They scare the buffalo. I believe when the sun rises they will come again."

"Why?" Harbaugh questioned.

"To kill us," Creek responded without emotion. "These Indians make deal with those we follow."

"Who worked that out?" Harbaugh asked.

"Possibly the driver of the wagon or perhaps Brunston himself," said Finnegan.

Harbaugh considered the matter for several moments. "Then do you suppose the Indians told them about us?"

"Yes, they saw us on the river," Creek explained.

"I'm sure they did," Finnegan said. "And I'm also sure Brunston made a deal with them to kill us."

"I just had a terrible thought," said Harbaugh. "Do you suppose Major Brunston is involved with the Indians?"

"Involved how?" asked Finnegan.

"Someone has been giving the Sioux guns," said Creek. "This I know to be true."

"And who better than an officer with connections?" said Finnegan.

They returned to the canoe and made plans. When finished, they set out their blankets and ate a supper of biscuits and dried jerky. The prospect of what awaited them at first light precluded any thoughts of sleep.

CHAPTER TEN

Sergeant Phelps led his horse up the rise of the Omaha ferry landing and tethered it to a hitching rail in front of a large log building. He paused to slap the dust from his clothing, then climbed a tier of plank steps and went inside. At the sound of the door closing, a man standing behind a counter ceased his paperwork and smiled.

"Howdy, Sergeant," he said. "What can I do for you?"

"I need to telegraph some messages."

"Well, you've come to the right place." He gestured to a nearby room. "Urgent, is it?"

"Yes sir." Phelps took the papers from inside his jacket and handed them over.

The man read the messages, shaking his head all the while. "Looks like you've had a heap of trouble," he said. "These kidnappers heading up the Platte?"

"Yes sir."

"Good Lord have mercy," the man said, continuing to shake his head. "I don't think you should worry none about catching them."

"How come?"

"Indians," the man responded. "Why, the entire Sioux nation is on the warpath. Even some Cheyenne have been seen down this way. They've been getting guns from somewhere—renegades, I reckon. Ain't safe for man nor beast west of here. Believe me, young fella, those kidnappers are doomed."

"Yes sir. Now could you see to sending those messages?"

The man started toward the telegraph, only to halt en route. "Last year, nearly a thousand warriors attacked Camp Rankin. Bands of Indians are raiding all up and down this part of the country," he said, his manner solemn. "With all due respect, you've got your work cut out for you."

CHAPTER ELEVEN

Dawn gradually diluted the dark shadows of night and gave definition to the endless stretch of land which confronted them. Fatigue weighed heavily on Finnegan while he waited for morning. He found sleep impossible. He lay atop the cabin of the gutted keelboat, pistol in hand. Off to his left, Harbaugh hunkered down behind a thick cottonwood. Creek lay behind a large log. Their plan was simple. Wait for the war party to attack and catch them in a crossfire.

The first rays of sunshine revealed the presence of buffalo a hundred yards away. Something was driving them straight to the river. It had to be the same group of Indians. Soon they heard shrill calls that became a deafening chorus. Buffalo charged wildly, panting and grunting, their pounding hooves setting up a thunderous rumble.

Finnegan watched the huge bodies crash through the tree line and plunge, bawling, into the water, violently rocking the charred hull of the keelboat. He peered through the rising dust for a glimpse of the enemy. Suddenly, a horse trampled a cluster of brush nearby and a figure vaulted onto the deck.

There was a dull thump followed by the scuffling of feet.

Finnegan held his fire and waited. The Indian surged forward, knife in hand. Clint's pistol barrel slammed his assailant full in the face and sent him sprawling backward onto the blackened boards. Before the Indian could rise, the Colt barked and the brave stiffened. He fell heavily, blood gushing from a chest wound.

Pandemonium prevailed. Gunshots mingled with the shrill screaming of horses. Finnegan wheeled around to see an Indian rushing him with an upraised club. He hurriedly squeezed off a round but missed. They went down in a struggle, hands clutching wrists. Clint's gun clattered out of reach. Rolling across the deck, they clawed and flailed at one another. Warm spittle from the Indian's mouth half blinded Finnegan as he struggled desperately to prevent the club from battering his skull. Angered, he butted his opponent on the crest of his nose and was rewarded with an anguished cry. He quickly pressed his advantage by kneeing his adversary. Another howl of pain followed and now he felt resistance wane.

Finnegan jammed his hand under the Indian's chin and pushed hard. He wrestled the club from the iron-like grasp. With all his might, Clint brought the heavy weapon down on the warrior's skull. Abruptly the battle was over.

Finnegan searched for the fallen pistol. He retrieved it, rested for a moment, and looked around him. The noise and shooting had stopped. Cautiously he climbed the embankment to see Harbaugh grappling with an Indian holding a knife. A well-placed bullet saved the lieutenant.

"Where's Creek?"

"I...I don't know," came the faint response.

Harbaugh was pale and listless. On closer inspection Finnegan noticed that one of his jacket sleeves was torn and sodden with blood.

"Get cut?"

"Afraid so," said Harbaugh.

Kneeling, Finnegan ripped away the sleeve and examined the wound. Taking a bandanna from his pocket, he firmly bound the ugly gash. "Wait while I check on Creek?"

"Sure. And thanks for the help."

Finnegan patted Harbaugh's shoulder. Reconsidering, Clint went through the lengthy process of reloading the Colt cap and ball. He scanned the trees and brush around him before hurrying across a clearing. Seeing movement, he dropped down and leveled the revolver.

"Don't shoot, Fire Canoe Finnegan," said a familiar voice.

"Are you all right, Creek?"

Branches parted to reveal the scout. "Come see," he said, and promptly disappeared.

Muttering to himself, Finnegan threaded his way to another opening in the dense undergrowth. There Creek had four Indian ponies, reins tied together and to a single tree. A few yards away a pair of legs protruded from under a bush.

"Can you ride with no saddle?" Creek asked.

"Yes, I did it quite a few times during the war."

"What about the lieutenant?"

"He'll have to," Finnegan answered. "But he's going to need some help."

"Trouble?"

"He's got a deep slash on his arm. Lost a lot of blood."

"Let me see."

Creek gathered the reins of the horses and led them to where Harbaugh lay. He tied the mounts to a thick sappling. Squatting, the Scout carefully loosened the bandanna and examined the wound. "Must take him to the river," he said.

Finnegan raised Harbaugh to a sitting position. "Lieutenant," he said. "I'll have to move you."

Harbaugh groaned.

As gently as possible Finnegan lifted the officer and carried him to a grassy place beside the water. Creek returned to the river and began to examine the lieutenant's wound.

Four dead from the war party, Finnegan thought. But there have to be others. No doubt they'll be back with help before much longer. Then he remembered Harbaugh's service revolver. He began walking through the thick grass in an ever widening circle. Several minutes passed before he came onto the Colt lying in some weeds. He hurriedly wiped the pistol against a pant leg and slipped it inside his belt.

The Indian ponies attempted to graze and weren't in the least skittish when Finnegan approached them. He ran his hand over the lean and well-muscled flanks of a dapple gray. All the while a broad-chested dun eyed him closely with quick, abrupt motions of its head. The other two horses were a bay and a chestnut. Each had a brand on its flank. These four were not Indian ponies but had been stolen from some outpost.

It was the bay that particularly interested him. From a strap around its neck hung a rifle housed in a brightly beaded scabbard trimmed with feathers. Clint removed the weapon with care and found it to be a Henry repeater. So how did a bunch of Indians get their hands on such a rifle? He replaced the weapon in the scabbard.

Finnegan went to the wagon tracks and dropped to one knee for a closer look. Then he examined the impression of a thick boot heel. This must have been a planned meeting.

From the direction of the river, a bull buffalo grunted loudly. The animal repeated its bellowing call. The horses nervously snorted and neighed. Clint ran to them, trying to reassure the upset animals.

"What's frightening them?" asked Finnegan. Then he noticed the ground beneath his feet begin to vibrate. His gaze followed those of the ponies in the direction of the plain and he saw clouds of dust rising. A large herd of bison were stampeding toward them.

Finnegan ran to the river bank. Harbaugh sat erect. Cloth strips encircled his wounded arm. He was naked to the waist, as his shirt had been shredded to fashion a bandage.

The bull bellowed once more.

Creek pointed to the rising dust on the plains. "Stampede!" he yelled. "We have to run for it."

Finnegan lifted Harbaugh to his feet and carried him up the embankment toward the startled horses. Creek ran past them and grabbed their possessions, packed in a canvas sack. The on-rushing herd stretched before them as far as the eye could see.

With the scent of buffalo strong in their nostrils, the horses were near panic. Finnegan had all he could do to get Harbaugh and himself mounted. Creek secured the provisions to the back of one horse and got astride another with the ease of one born to the task.

"Hang on!" Finnegan shouted.

Harbaugh merely nodded, his face ashen.

Drawing alongside, Creek pointed up river. Holding the reins of the second horse, he let out a loud whoop and dug his heels into the sides of his mount. The chestnut bolted into action as did the others until they were at a full gallop. The charging buffalo came ever closer, a bawling thundering mass that could not be withstood.

From his precarious perch on the back of the frantically racing bay, Finnegan saw they couldn't hope to outdistance the fast-closing herd. If the huge animals were not shunted aside in some manner, then death was inevitable. He reached for the rifle butt and withdrew the Henry repeater. Now the buffalo were so close their heads and horns could be clearly discerned.

He selected one of the great beasts, aimed, and shot. The Henry bucked in his hand. The buffalo turned its nose but kept right on course. A second shot caused it to stumble momentarily. The next bullet glanced off the beast's horns and the huge animal lurched to the side and fell. A large bunch of running animals tripped over the dead body, rolled, and fell. A quick succession of shots and more buffalo tumbled and died. The nearest running animals veered toward the center of the herd.

It was enough of a deflection to allow the four horses to skirt the outer edge of the stampede. A number of the buffalo shouldered close against Finnegan's mount and nearly unseated him. In a few terrible moments, the threat of total annihilation was over. The horses kept galloping through the choking dust, fear still driving them. Not until some distance had passed did they break pace and gradually slow to a trot.

Harbaugh had collapsed so that his head hung down, his body bouncing loosely with the bay's every stride. Finnegan held him by his arm to prevent him from falling while Creek got control of the reins.

"We'd better stop and care for him and rest the horses," Finnegan said.

Creek indicated a cluster of cottonwoods near the river. Not waiting for a reply, he cut off in that direction and Finnegan brought up the rear. They stretched Harbaugh out on a patch of shaded grass and placed a blanket under his head. The wound had stopped bleeding. Harbaugh was desperately in need of rest and water.

"I'll go scout." Creek swung his arm in a wide arc. "You fill the canteens. I will find a better place to camp and hide. I think we will stay until the lieutenant gets better and can ride."

Finnegan nodded. He took Harbaugh's pistol from his belt and handed it to Creek. Creek rode off toward the west. Finnegan watched him go and worried if this delay would ruin their chances to find Elisha. Perhaps it was already too late for the lieutenant.

CHAPTER TWELVE

Elisha sat quietly. By her own admission, she had cried enough. The eastern schoolgirl smugness was gone, a victim of the harsh realities of life and death in this wilderness. Already she had witnessed two gruesome murders and surmised Brunston had killed the third payroll robber. The prospect of more violence was likely. She was a helpless pawn. The young woman sat in an underground room with lengths of timber shoring up its earthen walls. A flickering candle provided the only light. It was as though she was entombed—buried alive.

Thoughts of Clint Finnegan and Lieutenant Harbaugh crept into her mind. Then she dismissed them as just an exercise in futility. Major Brunston told her the Sioux had seen both men and a scout paddling up the Platte. It wasn't any good to get her hopes up, because the Indians were going to ambush them. He had told her that before noon their scalps would be hanging in the sun to dry.

Elisha was afraid—more afraid than she had ever been in her young life. She had experienced danger before, but not like this. There were times during the war when the Confederates came so precariously close to the family home that she and her mother were forced to flee. Once they hid in a dense woods for two full days and nights without food or water. And she remembered being very scared. But she hadn't been alone—never had she felt so desperately alone as now.

"Cheer up, Miss Parkinson, we're going to have company today," said Brunston. "Very distinguished company."

Elisha gave a start, not realizing that the major was now standing in the doorway. He grinned at her in that sardonic way of his, like a cat playing with a canary which ultimately was destined to become a meal. She shuddered.

"You'll want to wash your face and put on a pretty smile," he said.

Brunston wore a loose-fitting shirt of coarse material and buckskin leggings. She took note of this change in dress and felt anger rising within her.

"Finally got rid of your uniform, I see," she said. "That's only fitting because you don't deserve to wear it. You're a traitor, and I hope someday you'll hang."

Without a word or so much as a change of expression Brunston came over and slapped her hard. She turned, tears welling up in her eyes.

"Best watch your mouth, young lady," he said. "I'm not a real patient sort."

Her lips thinned to an almost imperceptible line but she didn't break down. Instead she threw back her head with an air of defiance and avoided his gaze.

"Now get tidied up," he said. "And be quick about it." He pointed to the doorway. "Use the mirror in my room."

She preceded him down a narrow, darkened passageway. At its far end they emerged into a kitchen of sorts where the wagon driver named Witt sat on a stool, sipping the contents of a battered metal cup. He watched her closely. She hated the way he looked at her. It was a lingering possessive gaze that made her feel cheap and dirty. He had a swarthy complexion with a prominent nose. His broad shoulders and large hands suggested the presence of strength.

She followed Brunston to his room and stood before her reflection. The image in the cracked mirror elicited a sigh of dismay. Red-rimmed eyes stared back at her and one cheek still bore the mark of the major's slap. Her hair was a mess. She ran her fingers through the matted thatch with little effect.

"Use this," said a deep voice.

Reflected in the mirror was Witt. He held up a wooden comb. She accepted it. He merely grunted and left.

The homemade object worked well enough. While she combed her hair she heard Brunston's voice.

"Here they come."

Immediately there was the hasty scraping of stool legs on the rough board floor, accompanied by shuffling feet. Elisha hesitated, then peeked from the doorway. The kitchen was empty. She crossed to the passageway which led to the exterior of the cave-like structure. There she moved to a position near the entrance and peered out. She saw a number of Indians sitting astride horses.

Her gaze settled on a warrior who seemed to be their leader—a tall, powerfully built man. He wore only a buckskin vest, breechcloth, and leggings. A collection of bear claws attached to a thong encompassed his neck. Brunston and Winthrup stood before him while Witt hung back. Elisha listened closely to their conversation.

"Welcome, Hump," Brunston said. "Light down, if you want."

The Indian shook his head and looked around. "Did you bring more guns?"

"We're expecting a shipment," said the major. "But, I've got a little surprise for you." Brunston went to a canvas covering, pulled it back, and revealed fifteen Springfields. "Consider these rifles a gift."

Hump signaled and several warriors dismounted, gathered the rifles, and stepped back to their horses.

"For the future," said Brunston, "how are your people fixed for trade?"

"We have plenty of hides," Hump replied. "How soon will you bring more guns?"

"In just a few days," Brunston said.

"We need new repeaters," said the chief.

"We have mostly single-shot Springfields," said Winthrup. "They are accurate rifles used in the late war. It's hard to get Henrys."

Hump nodded. "Repeaters are better to fight the bluecoats."

"These weapons will suit your needs," said Brunston. "You're going to have your hands full. More soldiers are being sent to the forts to guard the territory. They'll have no repeating rifles, only single shots."

"We are many." Hump scowled. "Sioux, Cheyenne, Arapaho. Since Sand Creek our enemies no longer make war with one another. Now we are one." He held a finger aloft. "All of us fight the soldiers. We will stop the iron horse."

"From what I've heard, the old chiefs don't want to fight," Winthrup said. "They'd just as soon pass the peace pipe."

"Too late for peace. Every young warrior knows he must fight or die." Hump raised a clenched fist. "The intruders kill our buffalo, cut open our land, and kill us. So we must kill them. Our people understand this."

"The guns and ammunition we bring will help you," said the major.

A brief interlude of strained silence ensued before Hump said, "You stole from the fire canoe?" He gestured to Brunston. "Army scout and bluecoat follow. You make trouble for gun trade?"

"If they come, I have something to bargain with." Brunston turned and called to Witt. "Get the girl."

Elisha withdrew from the cave entrance, suddenly sick with fear. Then Witt's hand was on her arm.

"Company wants to meet you," he said.

She started to resist and felt his grip tighten.

"If you value your life, you will come with me," he said quietly. "The major wants to look big in front of the chief."

She resisted and Witt pushed her toward a grinning Brunston and a somber Winthrup. Hump peered intently at her.

"Meet Miss Elisha Parkinson," Brunston said. "Colonel Ambruster Parkinson's daughter. The colonel is stationed at Fort Randall."

Hump dismounted and approached her. He seemed even larger up close. She looked past him but was only too aware of his piercing gaze. After a moment he returned to his horse. When he was mounted again, he spoke Sioux to his companions. They laughed as though enjoying a joke.

"Send up smoke when you bring guns," Hump exclaimed.

"Will do, chief," Brunston replied.

Lifting an arm, Hump wheeled around and galloped off with his warriors in close pursuit. After they were gone, Witt led Elisha back to the house while Brunston and Winthrup stayed behind to talk. Once inside, she went directly to her room. Elisha sank down onto her cot, realizing just how serious her situation was. Some minutes passed before she heard movement, she turned to see Witt standing in the doorway.

"Hungry?" he asked.

"No."

"The chief liked you."

"I didn't like him." She looked away. "What did he say to the other Indians?"

"I don't know," answered Witt.

"You're lying. I don't believe you. I want to hear it."

Witt shrugged, "The chief said you were going to be one of his warrior's women."

Eyes widening, she started to speak, then thought better of it. She bit her lip instead.

"Chief Hump is strong medicine, a great warrior. All the other Indian leaders respect him."

"I don't care who he is," she said. "He can't give me away."

Witt nodded. "If you won't be a squaw then you're not going to live very long." He drew a finger across his throat in a cutting motion.

She covered her face with both hands.

"Sure you're not hungry?" When there was no reply, Witt shrugged his shoulders, and left.

CHAPTER THIRTEEN

Colonel Parkinson read the communiqué he received that afternoon, one more time. It was true. There could be no mistake. His daughter had come west and now she was kidnapped off the steamboat and in Indian territory.

Parkinson got up from behind his desk and walked to a window overlooking the parade grounds. He looked out but did not see what was before him. The images registering in his thoughts were from another military post. Ever so clearly he saw Elisha playing on the back step of a lieutenant's modest quarters. She was a beautiful child, so enthusiastic and inquisitive. From the outset he had vowed to protect her from the dangers inherent to military life. And he had succeeded, in spite of her willful behavior, until now.

Parkinson left the window and moved over to a wall where the portraits of two women hung beside one another. Elisha displayed an impish grin, so indicative of the spirit that characterized her youth. The other picture was of a more mature woman. Melissa, his wife, had endured much during his military career—always without complaint. Then, just when they were looking forward to his retirement and a quiet existence in the northeast, death took her away. It was as if a light had been extinguished in his life. Now the sole remaining source of brightness was his daughter. He must do everything within his power to rescue her.

The reflection in the mirror portrayed a gray-haired man a bit gaunt and worn in appearance. However, his eyes gave mute testimony to the intensity with which he still pursued life.

An old scout and mountain man once spoke of the colonel as being no more than a chew of jerk beef with bowed legs. This was accurate. Colonel Parkinson could still ride for hours alongside the youngest men in the troop. If he could, he would command the expedition to rescue his daughter. But, was she still alive? He had raised her to be no wall flower and if there was a way for her to survive, she would find it. A knock at the door interrupted his reverie.

"Come in," he said.

An officer entered and saluted.

"Major Trask, reporting as ordered, sir!"

"At ease, Major." Parkinson responded in kind and then motioned the officer to a chair.

"It's my understanding, sir, that my orders are to help you plan an expedition. I've brought the information you requested."

"Does post commander, Major Dryer, know of my daughter's kidnapping?" asked Colonel Parkinson.

"Yes sir, he does.

"He understands that according to my special orders, Washington assigned me to look into the Indian problem?"

"Yes sir, to some extent, but he asked me to have you clarify and report back to him," responded Major Trask.

"Specifically, Major, I am here by orders of the general staff to determine what tribes are aggressors, and to document hostiles and their numbers. My orders are to act independently, without interference.

"Yes sir, Colonel."

"Currently," continued Parkinson, "we are in defiance of the Fort Laramie Treaty wherein the Powder River country was given to the Sioux, Arapaho, and Cheyenne. The increased traffic of emigrants along the Oregon, California, and Bozeman trails are in violation of that treaty. The fact is, the Indians are fighting for their land, their hunting grounds, and their way of life."

"But, sir, it is our divine destiny to..."

"Off the record, Major Trask, we are the aggressors, and there is nothing divine about it. We have insufficient soldiers to stop the Indian raids. But, still, Washington wants the depredations to stop. I have brought a special troop of twenty soldiers and Lieutenant Robard. With these men I plan to go after the Army payroll and attempt to rescue my daughter. At the same time, I will be carrying out my orders to assess Indian tribes. Do you have the map, Major Trask?"

Trask spread the map atop the desk and Parkinson placed a forefinger on the spot designating Fort Randall. From there he traced a route almost due south to the North Platte.

"From here to there as the crow flies is just how far, Major?"

"Our scouts says it's a good two hundred miles."

"And from Fort Kearny to the mouth of the Platte?"

"About the same, sir," replied Major Trask.

Parkinson nodded, his eyes remaining on the map. "So, about a seven day march. What about the terrain?"

"Gently rolling pasture land for the most part," Trask replied. "The exception is right there, sir." He indicated a drawn circle. "That's a stand of trees. It's rather dense in parts, I'm told."

"Almost directly in our line of march?"

"Yes sir."

"Just the place for an ambush, I would suspect?"

"Yes sir."

"That leaves us no choice then," said Parkinson. "We'll simply have to avoid it. What is the best alternative route?"

"Several miles to the west, sir. On the way there's a small promontory. After that everything levels out quite nicely."

"What's the situation with water?"

Trask fingered another pencil mark. "The second day of the march you'll come to a small lake north of the forest area. Deer and buffalo drink there. If you boil the water for the men, it should be all right."

"And the next location?"

"Southeast of the woods is another small lake."

Parkinson bent over the map. "How far in that direction?"

"I'd say a few miles. A detail can get the water that you will need along the way with only a slight delay."

Parkinson nodded. "So nothing more than a Sunday stroll, if it weren't for the Indians?"

"Yes sir."

"And, our overall intelligence?" asked Parkinson.

Trask took a sheath of papers from under his arm and rapidly sorted through them.

"Our scouts to the north report heavy Indian activity," the major said. "Some of our soldier details have seen sizable groups of Sioux, Cheyenne, and Arapaho moving in this direction. As you know, woodcutting details are harassed almost daily at most of the forts and we are losing men..."

"And to the south?"

"There are quite a number of war party sightings, some as close as five miles from Omaha," explained Trask. "Boats pulling in there and at Council Bluffs report seeing Indians all up and down the Missouri."

"Major," said Parkinson. "Explain to Commander Dryer that according to General Sherman's headquarters in St. Louis, trappers and fur traders claim that the entire Indian nation east of the Rockies is astir. You can blame that on Chivington's massacre at Sand Creek. Tribes that were deadly enemies are now working together. The conflict is going to escalate, and I'll wager it will increase with the continued laying of tracks across Indian land and all the problems it brings with it."

Trask thought for a moment before inquiring, "Do you think twenty men will be sufficient for the trip?"

"I do not. However, I have already sent several communiqués to General Sherman. He has arranged for a cavalry detachment of fifty troops from Fort Kearny to join us en route. All they need to know is our line of march and a starting date so a rendezvous can be arranged." Parkinson pointed a finger to a spot on the map. "Looks like just south and west of the forest land would be our best place to meet."

"Yes sir. And I don't mind saying I'm relieved to know that you'll be reinforced."

"From the way things are shaping up, so am I."

"Perhaps I shouldn't ask, but do they know in Washington about this kidnapping and theft, sir?"

"No, and God willing they won't until the matter is satisfactorily resolved. If there are any problems, I'll worry about them when the time comes." He rolled up the map. "You'd better send that message to Fort Kearny now, Major. Just keep it short and sweet—departure time, the route, the size of our force, and so forth. Be specific as to our rendezvous point and that we will meet them seven days from today."

"Yes sir."

"Direct it to the attention of Captain C. L. Tyler. He's the officer in command at Fort Kearny."

"Very well, sir."

The colonel nodded. "Thank you, Major."

"My pleasure, sir."

"On your way out, tell the officer of the day to have my troops assembled as quietly as possible," said Colonel Parkinson. "I don't want to advertise our departure. I need to talk with my men before they begin making preparations for the march."

"Yes sir."

When Trask was gone Parkinson returned to the picture of his wife and daughter. He retreated a step and gazed at the portraits for a long moment. "God, if you can, look over Elisha and keep her safe until I find her." Then he turned, took his hat from the desk, and went out. Even as the door closed behind him he could hear footsteps and his troops assembling.

CHAPTER FOURTEEN

Harbaugh was unconscious and only a weak pulse could be detected. Finnegan tried to give him some water but most of it ran down from the corners of his mouth. Clint replaced the cork in the canteen. Then, from the north, he heard a rider coming.

Creek returned and insisted they move away from the river. The army scout had found a rocky area that led into a low depression. There they set up camp.

"This delay may ruin our chances to find the girl," said Clint. "Maybe I should…"

"It is best we stay together," said Creek. "What may come, I do not know, but you need me, and this man dies if we move him now."

Harbaugh lay near death and after five days he improved only slightly. Despite the urgency of their quest, Finnegan realized they couldn't leave the wounded lieutenant behind. On the fifth day they decided to head west and follow along the river to Fort Kearny.

If Creek hadn't the skill to build a travois, the lieutenant would likely be dead. Riding a horse would have certainly killed him.

The sun was lowering in the sky and the afternoon was waning. Creek was out scouting ahead. Finnegan estimated there were only a few hours of daylight left. Most of the afternoon had been spent following the five day old wagon tracks that seemed to also follow the Platte in a westerly direction. Because of the wounded lieutenant, they traveled very slowly. No signs of life were seen except for an occasional herd of buffalo. It was providence that their course followed the river. As Finnegan contemplated the futility of their task, he heard in the distance the persistent thud of hoof beats. He slipped the Henry from its scabbard and retreated to the protection of a nearby brush line. Within a few moments Creek approached at a gallop.

"I found a settler's camp," he said, reining to a halt.

"Where?"

"About two miles to the north."

"Anybody around?"

Creek shook his head.

"Good," Finnegan said, "let's make for it."

With Creek riding point, he led two mounts by the reins. The forth horse pulled the travois and Finnegan walked beside it. Clint kept the Henry in hand, eyes alert. Just as dusk was descending, they cleared a rise and came upon a strange sight.

A spacious tent comprised of buffalo hides flanked one side of a lean-to. Near it was a sod house and beside that was a large wagon with a torn bonnet. Tethered to a tree stump, a wolf dog growled menacingly. A crude wooden fence encompassed this curious settlement. The only means of entrance was a narrow gate and dirt path.

"Holy Hannah!" exclaimed Finnegan, as Creek dismounted. "What do you make of this?"

Before Creek could reply there was a rustle behind them.

"Don't nobody move," a rasping voice commanded. "All right, young fella. Shed that rifle nice and easy."

Finnegan did as instructed.

"That's real fine. Now, hands on your head, the two of you."

A large man came forward to confront them, a Henry repeater at the ready. In the failing light he assumed an almost supernatural appearance. Perched atop his massive head he wore a deerskin hat adorned with buck antlers. From beneath it spewed an unruly thatch of gray hair. Intense eyes peered at them from under bushy brows.

Finnegan's gaze was drawn to the body of an Indian draped over the horse's neck like a sack of meal.

"Looks like the soldier boy there is doing poorly," their captor said.

"He's near death," Finnegan replied. "We came here for help."

The man nodded. "Indians?"

"Yes. A war party attacked us."

For a long moment the man studied Creek. "He a friend of yours?"

"Uh-huh," Finnegan replied. "He's an army scout."

"You a soldier?"

"Nope. Assistant master of a steamer."

The man frowned. "One of them paddleboats?"

"Yes."

"How in thunder did you get this far off the water?"

"I'm after some people who stole an army payroll from my boat," Finnegan explained. "We followed them up the Platte River by canoe until they went to ground. That's when the Indians hit us."

"Got some of their stolen army horses, I see. So you must have done all right."

Finnegan nodded. "Except for the lieutenant."

"Well, let's get him help." The man motioned them toward the path. Take your horses as well as the travois."

Creek gathered the reins of three mounts and Finnegan led the horse pulling the lieutenant. They went ahead and the big man retrieved Finnegan's Henry. As they neared the building, the wolf dog snarled viciously and strained at its leash.

"Shush up!" the man said and the animal cowered.

In passing through the fence, Finnegan noticed a number of scalps hanging from a pole in the inner yard. He thought of the dead Indian and surmised his hair would soon be joining this collection.

"Don't mind hitching the ponies. The fence will keep them in."

Their captor indicated they should enter the soddy. When the heavy log door gave way they were greeted by a strong smell of cooking meat. It filled the stale atmosphere. Not until then did Finnegan fully realize there were no windows, either for ventilation or viewing. An aging Indian woman came to meet them. Her features betrayed no emotion at the arrival of unexpected guests. Only her eyes hinted at curiosity.

"This here's Pacho," the man said. "I can't pronounce her name so I call her that. She looks after things for me." He pointed to several buffalo hides piled on the floor. "Put the soldier boy there."

Finnegan and Creek went out and carefully lifted Harbaugh from the drag and carried him inside the building. The wounded man's skin was pale and clammy to the touch. Placing the lieutenant on the hides, Clint glanced at the woman. She waved him away.

"Pacho don't like anybody around when she's doing her work," the man explained. "No sense worrying about the soldier boy. If he's marked to live, ain't nothin gonna kill him. But if it's his time to go, then there ain't nothin gonna keep him here."

"There may be some truth to that," replied Finnegan.

He took a quick survey of his surroundings. The interior consisted of one great open space. Candles and a pair of oil lamps sat on barrels and storage crates. The only pieces of furniture were a large wooden table and three straight back chairs.

Underfoot was packed dirt except for the far end of the building where Harbaugh lay. A fireplace and hearth built of rough stones dominated the room. There a pot boiled over hot coals.

"Well, make yourself to home," the man said. "I've got to take care of that Indian yonder."

The man went outside and Finnegan joined Creek, who sat cross-legged in a corner watching Pacho minister to Harbaugh.

"I don't know what we've got ourselves into here," Finnegan whispered.

Creek tapped a finger to his head. "Old hair chin is loco," responded the scout in an equally soft voice. "Soon his scalp will be hanging in an Indian lodge."

"Possibly, but he survived this long. He doesn't seem particularly unfriendly. Maybe I can get him to talk and find out if he's seen Brunston and the others."

Pacho got up slowly and stared at Harbaugh for a time. "He sleeps," she said. "When he wakes, I'll give him more soup. It will make him strong."

Finnegan nodded. "We sure appreciate what you're doing."

"Do you eat?" she asked.

"It's been awhile."

She motioned to them and they followed her to the fireplace. "Deer and antelope," she said gesturing toward the simmering pot.

"Thank you, ma'am," Finnegan replied. "That will suit us just fine."

She pointed to the table and they sat down. When she brought the meat it was steaming hot and emitted a sweet, savory smell. She gave each of them a generous portion in a strangely shaped bowl. Then she brought forks and knives. They ate in silence for several minutes.

Only when Finnegan began to experience a sense of fullness did he become curious about the unusual shape of his bowl. He held it up for closer inspection. Both the inner and the outer surfaces were strangely smooth and of an odd color. Off to one side he could see Creek watching him.

"What do you suppose it is?" he whispered.

Creek made a wry face and shook his head.

Now Finnegan ran an appraising finger along the shallow ridges on the inside of the vessel. He looked up and his gaze encountered a human skull on a nearby barrel. The top of the head had been removed so a candle could be placed inside. After several seconds of contemplation he turned his plate over and laid it atop the skull. It proved to be a perfect fit. He glanced at Creek who stared back at him.

"Good Lord A'mighty!" he exclaimed. "We've been eating out of a skull cap."

"Loco," Creek responded solemnly.

Finnegan grabbed the skull cap just as the door opened to admit the big man. The fellow seemed to be in a jovial mood. The hunting knife he held was stained with blood. He dipped it in a bucket of water before going over to the Indian woman. They conversed in low tones.

"The soldier boy is doing right smart," he said placing the hat with the antlers on the table. "He's starting to pink up real nice."

"That's good to hear," Finnegan replied.

Creek gazed into space.

"You boys get enough to eat?"

"Sure did," said Clint. "And it tasted good."

The big man nodded and sat down heavily on one of the chairs.

Creek got to his feet. "Sleep," he said simply and turned away.

"Just grab some of them skins and bunk wherever it suits you," the man said.

Pacho brought the scalp hunter an ample serving of meat and he ate hungrily.

From hooded eyes Finnegan studied the skull cap dish. Then he thought about the bloody knife and the fact that another scalp must be drying on the pole outside.

"Comes to mind, we ain't become properly acquainted," the man said wiping his mouth with the back of a broad hand. "The name's Abner Mosely. Some folks call me Liver Eatin Mosely. That's cause I got a hankerin for liver. I like all kinds." He leaned on the table, a twinkle in his eye.

"You don't say," Finnegan replied, squirming uncomfortably.

"I cut them out of buffalo, antelope, bears and the like." He winked knowingly. "Some folks say I even cut them out of Indians."

"Uh, is…is that true," Finnegan stammered.

Mosely chuckled. "You bet I do!"

"Do…you eat them?"

"Nope."

"Then why...?"

Raising his hand, Mosely bellowed, "Let me go back to when…" He stopped abruptly and slapped his knee. "I'm right sorry to be so inhospitable. I flat forgot to ask your name."

"Finnegan. Clint Finnegan."

"I'm right pleased to meet you, Clint. To folks that know me personal, I answer to Ab."

"All right…Ab."

"Now then, I was going back to when I first come here. It'll be five years this summer as near as I can recollect. We was ridin in that old prairie schooner out yonder." He jerked a thumb in the direction of the wagon left to weather beside the building. "There was me and the wife and Little John, my boy. I left farmin in Kentucky to go west. Thought I'd pan and dig a spell, and see how things turned out. Some other folks was with us."

"Then you were ambushed?" asked Finnegan.

Mosely nodded his head. "Sioux attacked just south of Westport Landing in Kansas. Most everybody got burned out. The folks that survived headed for Fort Leavenworth. All save me. I was going to California or bust trying. So we kept on moving, looking to hook up with another wagon train. We wandered up this way when fever took hold of my wife. She was awful weak so I stopped here, thinkin we'd stay till the fever quit her. But she up and died, leavin me and the boy."

He closed his eyes in a prolonged silence.

"I'm real sorry to hear that," Finnegan said quietly.

With a sigh, Mosely stared at the flames in the hearth.

"I played the fool, and she done the paying," he said at length. "Little John wasn't but five. I took him everywhere, huntin, fishin, plantin. Why, I fixed a tent from hides and set it up alongside the wagon. We lived there. Early one mornin a war party jumped us. They cracked my head, stole the mules, and fired the tent. My boy was killed in the doing."

Mosely's face became an expressionless mask.

"That night I tracked them Sioux," he continued. "I found their camp up the river. They were butcherin one of my mules. Gonna make a meal of him. I killed them all and got my mules back. I've been goin at it ever since."

"Did you…take any livers?"

"Not directly." Mosely appeared to be at ease with himself now. "I commenced that later." He leaned across the table. "I learned about Indians from trappers traveling the river to Omaha. They told me what spooks them. And cuttin out their livers does that right proper. Scalpin does too."

"How do you mean spooks them?"

"Well, Indians don't like to lose parts. They believe you can't go to the spirit world if you ain't in one piece."

"So why do you hang those scalps on a pole?"

"They're hangin there for a purpose," Mosely explained.

"Aren't you baiting them?"

"That's the idea," Mosely said, his anger rising. "Young fella, this is a hard country. A man what don't look after himself is gonna be dead in a hurry." He gestured toward the woman. "She's Pawnee. Tells me her tribes been enemies with the plains Indians since the beginning of time. I come onto some Sioux trying to cut her up. Naturally I had to kill em."

"I see," said Finnegan.

"She's been grateful and a good friend ever since. I trust her more than I do myself."

"Do you mind telling me why you killed that Indian tonight?"

"Nope. It's because he's been trackin me for a spell."

"Tracking you?"

"That's a fact." Mosely paused to pluck a bit of gristle from between his teeth with a knife. "Like I been sayin, I've killed me quite a few Sioux. And they ain't happy about that. I got most of the warriors skeered of me. One of their chiefs named Hump took to sending his best after my hair. This fella I got tonight was one of them."

"Did you cut out his liver?"

"I did. And I tossed his body yonder over the fence. They'll drag it off come mornin."

"Wha...what did you do with the liver?"

"I gave it to the wolf. He eats them." Mosely grinned. "You look a bit pale, Clint. Off your feed, are you?"

"You're a hard man, Ab Mosely," said Finnegan. "So you cut their livers out just to spook them?"

"Yup, that I do. Hate those Indians that killed my son with a passion. Pacho feels the same. That's why I do it. I hear they claim I'm an evil spirit. To sum it up, they ain't real anxious to fret me none."

"I'm thinking you're lucky you lived this long."

"Tell the truth, I don't care one way or t'other."

"I have a question to ask you," said Finnegan.

"Go ahead."

"Did you happen to see the payroll thieves?"

"Maybe I seen them," said Mosely.

"Really?" Finnegan stiffened.

"I said maybe. Two men was they?"

"Yes."

"And a woman?" Mosely's eyes narrowed. "She one of the robbers?"

"No. They kidnapped her."

"Pretty is she?"

"Sure as the sun rises."

Mosely chuckled. "Could be you want to find her more than you do that payroll?"

Finnegan looked away and said nothing.

"Was one of them wearin an army uniform?"

"For certain. Major Avril Brunston. The other fella's name is Alonzo Winthrup."

"I seen em right enough," Mosely said. "The two men and the woman was ridin in a wagon with Witt

Deaver, a no-account gun-runnin half-breed. He's been sellin to the Indians around here for months. The army knows it, but can't never corral him."

"Got any idea where he hides out?"

Mosely shook his head. "But I'll lay you even, it ain't far off."

"Why do you say that?"

"Almost every day I see war parties headin north and east of here," Mosely replied. "Sometimes after dark I follow them. The tribes are gatherin to do somethin big."

"And Deaver's giving them guns?" asked Finnegan. "Tell me what you think."

Mosely pursed his lips. "I think Deaver's got a place where nobody pays much mind. Close to the river, where he can meet the boats bringin the guns."

"Where?"

"Some hidden place inland but not too far from the Missouri and the mouth of the Platte. That's where Deaver does business."

"You know that for a fact?"

"I do; I seen him once," explained Mosely. "At dark, boatmen bring the guns upriver and Deaver meets them with a wagon. Secrets them under a load of skins."

"What does Deaver take as pay?"

"Pelts, skins, and hides from the Indians. He sells them to eastern fur buyers. There's a lot of them tradin off the river."

"How did you learn this?"

"From watchin. The rest from askin questions over to the fort."

Finnegan showed surprise. "Are we close to Fort Kearny?"

"No, it's a good, hard, five day's ride west on the Platte."

"Five days!" exclaimed Finnegan. "We'll lose their trail. We can't wait that long."

Mosely got to his feet. "You can't go it alone, that scout and you. Besides, that soldier boy ain't goin nowhere. But sure as the sun rises, if you do, you'll both lose your scalps. Face it, you're gonna need help. Help against them Sioux and help findin Deaver's hideout and where they got that girl."

Finnegan rose to his feet and paced. "I don't like it, but I guess you're right. I'm afraid too much time has gone by already."

"We can start tomorrow morning," said Mosely. "You can tell them officers about the payroll thieves and the soldier boy there. I figure they'll listen closer to you than they do me."

"Why?"

Mosedly laughed. "They think I'm a mite touched in the head." His expression sobered. "Can't get them to listen or to understand a war's a brewin. It's simple figurin—the Indians got their land—and the whites want it. The whole Indian nation from the Missouri River to the Rockies is fixin to fight. Won't be long afore a white man's life ain't worth a chew and a spit." He stretched. "Well, guess I'll lay me down. First light ain't that far off."

"We'll need our guns," Finnegan said.

"Claim them when you're ready." Mosely pointed to the Henry and the two Colts which lay on a barrel top. "The way to the fort is right dead through Indian country. We're going to need all the guns we can muster."

"I think we better take Creek along."

Mosely grinned. "The only Indians I don't trust is the ones out to bury me. I got no trouble with Creek." He yawned. "Just grab some of them skins and roll up where it's convenient."

CHAPTER FIFTEEN

Young Lieutenant Cale Robard entered the Fort Randall commissary and stood off to one side of the door. He twice cleared his throat discreetly before an attractive girl working behind a nearby counter glanced up and noticed him. She smiled and came over.

"What are you doing off duty at this hour?" she asked, taking his hand in hers.

"I'm not off duty, honey," he replied. "We're getting ready to ride out and the colonel allowed the men a few minutes to say good-bye."

Her smile fading, the girl inquired, "Why didn't you mention anything about going away?"

"That's because I didn't know there would be an assignment until after we had talked," he explained. "It was kind of an unexpected thing. At least that's my understanding."

"Will you be gone long?"

"I can't be sure. A week or so. We're heading to the North Platte. I'm told it's a seven day ride if all goes well. But we're taking more rations than just a trip back and forth will require."

The girl looked concerned. "Is there some kind of trouble?"

He shrugged. "We're meeting a cavalry group from Fort Kearny."

"Oh, Cale, I'm so worried," she said.

"No need for that." He took her in his arms. "Do us good to get more field experience."

It was nearly time to go. The lieutenant held his young lady close and kissed her. Unnoticed, the Indian woman who was sweeping the floor withdrew to the back of the store. There she beckoned to a young boy who was playing outside. He came running and she spoke to him in a low tone. Nodding, he scampered off toward the parade ground even as the troops were gathering en masse.

With a practiced ease, the Indian boy weaved in and out of the horses and men while making his way to the main gate of the fort. He slowed to a walk until clear of the compound, then began running toward a small Sioux trade settlement near the stockade walls. Once among the tepees, he singled out an Indian who sat smoking a pipe. When the boy talked, the Indian listened quietly then got up and mounted a horse picketed nearby. He rode off leisurely at first, but once out of sight, quickly urged his mount to a full gallop.

CHAPTER SIXTEEN

The distant lights of Portsmouth reflected eerily off the night clouds and could barely be seen through the dark. Far to the south, Deaver guided the wagon through a patch of low ground. He smiled to himself. All had gone according to plan, so far. And he felt there was no reason to believe it wouldn't continue to do so. Only he wasn't one to take things for granted. In the calm night atmosphere he easily discerned the sound of rushing water and turned the horses toward it. Even as he did, his eyes were searching the distant shoreline for a familiar glint. Within a matter of minutes Deaver's wagon came to the North Platte. Not too far away, this river flowed into the great expanse of the Missouri River. Searching, he finally saw the gleam of a lantern almost magically drifting closer through the gloom. He breathed easier. The flatboat had made it past Fort Leavenworth and St. Joseph landings without being detected. Still, experience dictated that every precaution should be taken.

Deaver reined in the horses, set the brake, and removed a lantern which hung from a peg beside his seat. He raised the glass and lit the wick. Slowly and deliberately he swung the lamp to and fro, then waited for a response. Within a few moments he saw the light marking the position of the flatboat moving towards him. Satisfied, he set off for the rendezvous point along the shoreline. Reaching it, Deaver halted the wagon.

"Any trouble?" inquired Jack, a lean, bearded man standing at the bow of the boat along with three other men.

"Nope." Deaver got down from the wagon and waited, lantern in hand. "Let's get this done. I want to be shed of this place before dawn. I'm too close to Portsmouth as it is."

While they spoke, one of the men came forward and laid a plank between the boat and the bank, then crossed it. He approached until Deaver's upheld lantern defined his sullen features.

"Howdy, Will Scower," Deaver said. "Looks like you ain't fit company for man or beast, as always. Who rearranged your face?"

"Still trying to be the funny man, huh breed? Well, you don't show no improvement yourself."

Chuckling, Deaver walked up the ramp to the boat. "Let's see what you got, Jack," he said to the bearded man.

"Why sure. And we'll be having a peek at your wares."

"Peek all you want." Deaver swung an arm toward the wagon. "The buffalo skins on top are for cover, so leave them be. Everything else is fair game."

Jack motioned for his two accomplices to go to the wagon and examine its contents. When the two men left the boat, Jack took Deaver to the rear deck and drew back the corner of a large canvas which shrouded several wooden boxes. Deaver laboriously cut the binding on one of them and lifted its lid. From within he removed a .58 1861 Springfield rifle.

"Stolen?" he inquired.

The bearded man nodded. Going down on his haunches, Deaver examined the box lid.

"Springfield Armory," he read aloud. "You got contacts there?"

"Could be," Jack replied. "But I don't know for certain. And I ain't curious to find out. It's downright unhealthy. Them gents in the stiff shirts back east have ways of reaching a body even out here. A fella who was our supplier in Jefferson City got his hair parted a few days ago. Caught him with his fingers in the candy jar, I heard. He was messing with a shipment of Henrys."

Deaver replaced the rifle and secured the box lid. "Any Henrys in those other crates?" he questioned.

"Henrys are scarce, Springfields aren't. I brought you plenty of powder, minié balls, and caps."

"You didn't answer my question, I was promising the Indians a load of repeaters, not those old Civil War muskets," said Deaver.

"There's one crate of Henry repeaters and a few boxes of ammunition for them," replied Jack. "Who's gonna get them, some big chiefs?"

"It ain't for me to say." Deaver stood up. "When can we start loading?"

"Directly."

Jack went to meet his two associates who had returned from inspecting the wagon. He conversed with them briefly, then came back to Deaver.

"We'll stash the skins from your wagon first, then help with the guns," Jack said. "Fair enough?"

"I'll be watching."

Jack went ashore. Deaver wandered to the stern of the boat and peered down the river. The exchange was taking too long for his liking. He spit into the dark water and turned his thoughts to the rifles. Rifles of any kind in the hands of Hump and his warriors was an improvement over the bow and arrow. This meant a lot of white people were going get killed, some of them women and children.

Deaver looked back to the bow of the boat and saw the dark outline of Will Scower. For the bruiser he was, he sure seemed like a lazy man. Deaver turned to look out over the river and once again reflected on the effect this gunrunning business had on the tribes.

The soldiers kept coming along with the land-grabbers, continuously breaking treaties. It was said General Sherman advocated the killing of buffalo to eliminate the food supply. Word was spreading that the railroad would be continuing across the plains. Only trouble was, the white man had the fever. No matter if they were soldiers, settlers, miners, or railroaders—it was too late to stop them. They were going to leave a lot of tepees empty before this was over.

As the men laid the skins and the hides on the deck, Deaver turned his thoughts to his own prospects. It didn't really matter who won because he knew there wouldn't be anything for a breed. Neither side wanted him. They could only see the half that was hated. So why should he be concerned about selling guns to the Indians? It wasn't his fight one way or the other. And a man, even a breed, had to make a living.

They're going to war anyway, so I might as well get what I can and run for it. Head Northwest? Go by myself? His hands clenched into fists. *Take a wife? An Indian woman?*

He spit into the water, once more picturing the fresh-faced girl—the hostage. He knew Brunston and Winthrup were going to get rid of her once they were free of danger. And he also knew Hump planned to trade her off as revenge against the Army and the girl's father. He had heard the Sioux warrior say as much.

If I helped her to escape, would she be willing to be my woman? Likely not. But then again, I can ask her. What do I have to lose? Nothing. Absolutely nothing.

"Gonna give us a hand, breed?"

The antagonistic edge to Scower's voice cut sharply across Deaver's thoughts, severing them.

"Didn't know you would need help," he replied, grinning, knowing it irritated the bully. "Then again, I guess your kind always needs help."

Scower cursed and Deaver laughed.

By the time the boxes of rifles had been loaded, there was already a hint of gray on the horizon. Deaver viewed it with a deep sense of anxiety. First light was no more than a few hours away and he'd be hard pressed, particularly with the weight of his cargo, to make the distance up the Platte to his hideout.

"I'm going with you," growled Scower.

"No you're not," replied Deaver.

"I missed the boat at Fort Leavenworth; I need a ride to meet up with Brunson and collect my money."

"Then if you're going, keep your mouth shut and don't rile me."

Deaver had to make sure he avoided the army patrols. With the increase of Indian activity, the cavalry had begun conducting periodic scouting expeditions. He knew there was a federal reward for his arrest on gunrunning charges. Some energetic pony soldier would just love to collect it. To make matters worse, at the first sign of trouble, Scower would start shooting. He detested the man, not only because he was mean, but stupid as well, and therefore dangerous.

"How long's this gonna take?" Scower growled.

"Too long, if we don't get to my hideout before daybreak," said Deaver, whipping the horses.

Scower gripped the seat with both hands as the wagon lurched and began bouncing over the rough terrain. Giving a sidelong glance at his companion, Deaver wondered why Brunston and Winthrup would want such a lout around to share the payroll. Then it occurred to him that they simply intended to close his mouth permanently. He smiled and snapped the reins harder.

CHAPTER SEVENTEEN

Hump, the Miniconjou Sioux warrior, held a simmering piece of venison on a stick. Slowly he turned the hunk of charred meat in front of his face, eyes attentive to the glowing and sputtering embers of the fire before him, so mesmerized that he seemed not to be aware of the Indian entering the teepee behind him.

"A messenger is here," the Indian announced.

"Bring him," Hump said.

The warrior went out and Hump replaced the meat stick next to the fire. For several moments he continued to stare at the flames with a detached air. When the messenger entered, Hump stood to confront him.

"I come from Fort Randall."

Hump nodded. "Do the soldiers ride from there?" he asked the messenger.

"Yes, Chief."

"When?"

"Two suns ago."

"Where?"

"Towards the Platte and the big river."

"Why?"

The messenger shook his head. "I do not know."

"How many?"

In response, the Indian messenger opened and closed his two hands, widely spreading ten digits twice. "Maybe more," he added.

"Do they bring a big gun on wheels?"

"No, but supplies on horses."

After a long pause Hump laid a hand on the messenger's shoulder. "I want you to ride," he said. "Tell Crying Wolf and the council chiefs we will meet in four days."

The messenger nodded and hurried out. A few moments later Hump's advisor returned.

"What do you think, my friend?" he asked.

"It is clear the bluecoats ride to scout our land," Hump replied. "Once they finish, more whites will come. Did you speak with the messenger?"

The Indian nodded.

"Is it Colonel Parkinson who leads?"

"Yes."

"So, the opportunity for revenge comes to us," Hump watched the smoke rise from the fire. "He is the father of the fresh-faced squaw. We will be ready for them. The colonel and his soldiers must die in the same manner they have killed our people. It is just."

CHAPTER EIGHTEEN

Elisha lay on the blanket, eyes closed. She was not asleep as her posture indicated. Instead, she listened intently to the conversation taking place in the adjoining room. The words were thick with the influence of whiskey and belligerent in tone.

"I say we split the money now," Winthrup said.

"Why, what's the hurry?" Brunston replied. "Neither of us is going anywhere until we deal those guns to the Indians. As long as the money's in one place we can keep an eye on it."

"Maybe, but I'd rather take care of what's mine and you can look after what's yours. That way there's no hard feelings."

"Hard feelings?"

"Yes," Winthrup responded. "If something happens to your part, that's on you. If something happens to the whole pot, then one of us is going to feel mighty unhappy."

"Just what are you suggesting?" There was a decided edge to Brunston's voice.

"We left Woody and Lem lying dead back on that boat and they were to get a full share," Winthrup replied, "and that man—I didn't even know who he was—you dumped in the river. Back then you said their passing just meant a bigger cut for us."

"As I recall, you didn't argue the point."

"No, and I still don't. Will Scower is coming here and we've already agreed to shuck him first thing. So that leaves just you and me."

"Nothing new there."

"What an awful hunk of money," said Winthrup. "Especially if only one of us was to come by it."

"Have plans, do you?" Brunston inquired.

"No, I don't. I'm real satisfied with what's coming to me. But I'm not convinced you see it that way."

"Oh? Why do you say that?"

"It was you who planned to get rid of Woody and Lem from the outset," Winthrup said. "And it was you who decided Will Scower should be crossed off the list. Now I've been wondering if you haven't made up your mind to kill me."

"Couldn't I say the same thing about you?"

"You could, and that's why I want to remove all temptation before things get out of hand," said Winthrup. "So let's split now and be done with it."

"Then you've decided against going west with me?"

"Let's just say I thought better of it," Winthrup responded.

"A man alone out there won't last long."

"Maybe I'm not going out there."

"Then where are you heading?"

"Never you mind about that. Just haul the money box from under the bed and we'll get on with business."

There was a prolonged silence before Brunston said, "Well, if I can't change your mind..."

More silence ensued, then a scraping sound reached Elisha's ears as though something was being dragged across the board floor.

Suddenly Winthrup roared, "Oh, no you don't!"

Then came the resounding report of a gunshot, followed by a muffled thud. Elisha heard footsteps, then Brunston appeared in the passageway. He leaned against the door, a pistol in one hand. With effort, he righted himself and entered the room.

"Winthrup's dead," he said simply, "and I'm not done yet. So we'll just wait until Witt Deaver and Will Scower get back."

She stared at him, eyes wide with fear. After a terrifying interlude of several seconds, he turned away and staggered to the main room. There he settled into a chair and sat quietly.

"Oh dear God," she whispered, a clenched hand to her lips.

CHAPTER NINETEEN

Surrounding them were gently rolling plains that offered the viewer an unobstructed vista for miles. Lieutenant Cale Robard squinted at the sun, noting its position in the sky. They had been riding for seven days. It was past noon. He wore his hat a bit lower than regulations recommended to shield a complexion already ruddy and well freckled.

At the sight of the colonel's upraised arm, Robard quickly spurred his horse to the head of the column.

"Yes sir?"

"We'll break on that high ground," Parkinson said, indicating the area with a gloved hand. "Give the troops a chance to rest and water their horses. Once we're situated I want you and the noncoms to meet with me."

"Yes sir."

Robard saluted crisply, turned about, and galloped back along the line of march, dispensing the colonel's orders. In a matter of minutes the encampment was established. The lieutenant, two sergeants, and two corporals joined Colonel Parkinson.

"Gentlemen," said Parkinson. "I've waited until now to fully inform you of our mission. One is strategic and the other personal. If I had conducted this meeting at the fort, word of our purpose would surely have leaked out. Even now I believe we're being watched. Some of you have no doubt noticed the smoke along the way. I wouldn't be surprised if the hostiles already know our destination, near a forested area and not too far from the North Platte River. What they don't know is why we're going there."

He paused to spread a map on the ground. "Somewhere in this location along the Platte River are believed to be two or more men who have stolen an army payroll which was destined for Cow Island. Our belief is they plan to escape to either Oregon or California. We will be joining forces here with fifty soldiers from Fort Kearny. Together we will travel to the Platte and search for the thieves. Just how long this operation might be expected to last, I can't say. We could apprehend the fugitives in a matter of days or weeks."

Rolling up the map, Parkinson said, "I mentioned earlier having a personal interest in this mission. Simply put, the thieves abducted my daughter from the steamboat carrying the payroll and are holding her hostage. I'm informed also that an army officer name Harbaugh, his scout, and a steamboat crew member are also tracking the kidnappers. We have no idea where they are or if they're even still alive."

He looked to his men to see if they understood him.

"Adding to the difficulty of our task are the Indians. We've been hearing reports for months now informing us of their preparations for war. We are greatly outnumbered, so we must be cautious as we proceed. Any questions?"

When none were forthcoming, he continued.

"Make sure every man in your company has his weapon loaded and is ready to fight. When we reassemble I want the scouts at the head of the column." He studied the men's faces briefly. "Very well, gentlemen, you're dismissed."

Robard returned to his horse and stood patting its neck. There was a perceptible tightness in his stomach, not from fear but anticipation. The colonel gave the call to mount, and the lieutenant swung into the saddle.

CHAPTER TWENTY

Before dawn, Ab Mosely woke Finnegan and Creek. They rose to eat a breakfast of venison stew. Clint went to Lieutenant Harbaugh, who was still lying motionless on the buffalo hide. Even in the weak lantern light, the wounded man looked better.

"The woman will take care of him," said Mosely. "You said you were in a hurry—if we're going, we better git to it."

Finnegan and Creek followed the Indian fighter outside. Mosely had put together supplies and since they were missing two saddles, provisions for the trip were packed on one of the unshod mules. The animals were ready and waiting.

"It's not like Fort Kearny is around the corner," said Ab. "Maybe if we're lucky we'll run into an army patrol and can convince them to join us."

The three men rode out on the tough mustangs, Mosely up front and Finnegan leading the mule. They traveled a few miles before the sun began to rise. It was Mosely who spotted movement on the open plain, and they stopped to observe.

"Got me this spyglass," said the self-made frontiersman, pulling it from his pocket.

"What do you see?" asked Clint.

"We're in luck; somebody musta been prayin. It's an army patrol, and I figure them soldier boys are from Fort Kearny."

"A good sign for all of us," said Creek.

"Finnegan, how do you want to play this?" asked Mosely. "Won't do to get shot."

"Ride in on them in the open?"

The party of three took their four animals and rode in plain sight straight for the moving column of soldiers.

A captain and an Indian scout met them ahead of the troops. They stopped their horses and the soldiers behind halted. The captain cautiously considered the approaching riders.

"Hello, Captain," said Clint. "We've been riding for Fort Kearny, we've got..."

"We're from the fort," said the officer, his eyes assessing the three men, their mounts, and equipment. "What do you want?"

"Can't fool me, Captain Tyler," said Mosely, pushing his mount closer. "Boys, meet the post commander of Fort Kearny."

"Indian killer," said the captain's scout, spitting out the words. "Liver Eatin Mosely."

"That's me all right. Captain, it would go well if you listened to this man."

"Speak your piece," said the captain. "We're pressed for time. And you are...?"

"Clint Finnegan, assistant master of the Dakota Dawn."

"The Dakota Dawn?"

"It's a steamboat."

"Yes, of course." The captain looked to the others. "And who are these men?"

"The name's Abner Mosely. You remember me, I got a little spread down the river a piece."

"And this is Creek," Finnegan explained, "He's an army scout."

"I see." The captain studied Finnegan. "Just what is the nature of your business?"

"We'd like to talk about the army payroll that was stolen from my boat," Finnegan explained.

"The Dakota Dawn?"

"Correct."

"Your steamboat was transporting this payroll... where?"

"To the garrison at Cow Island."

Attentive now, the captain asked, "You witnessed the robbery?"

"Yes."

"Who took the money?"

"Major Avril Brunston, a civilian named Alonzo Winthrup, and three other accomplices who are unidentified," Finnegan replied. "They escaped on a keelboat up the Platte River. We pursued them."

"You, Mr. Mosely and the scout?"

"No. Myself, Creek, and Lieutenant Ferris Harbaugh."

"Where is the lieutenant?"

"Recovering from a wound received in an Indian attack."

The captain shook his head. "This is all very confusing."

"Lookee here, Captain," said Mosely. "We got a pretty fair idea where the payroll thieves are holed up."

"And every minute we spend talking could cost Elisha Parkinson her life," Finnegan added.

Frowning, the captain asked, "Just who is Elisha Parkinson?"

"The only daughter of Colonel Ambruster Parkinson, special officer assigned at Fort Randall," Finnegan said. "She was taken captive during the payroll robbery."

"All right, all right," the captain said, holding up his hand in a restraining fashion. "It seems to me this is definitely a matter we should discuss."

Captain Tyler raised his arm and a sergeant rode briskly forward.

"Twenty minute break, Sergeant," ordered the captain. "Maintain silence, no talking in the ranks."

"Yes sir!" replied the sergeant, and he returned to the troops and quietly passed down the orders, and the soldiers began dismounting to stand or sit, holding reins.

The captain got off his mount and beckoned with a finger. "Come with me, gentlemen."

Finnegan, Creek, and Mosely also dismounted and the captain's scout took the reins of the horses while the Fort Kearny commander led the three men to a copse of cottonwoods and a large fallen tree. Captain Tyler immediately sat down.

"Didn't want my men to see me rest, but it's been a hard six-day ride so far and it's been some time since I've been out on patrol and... Well, keep talking Mr. Finnegan, you have my attention."

"What do you want me..." began Finnegan, and the captain interrupted.

"I've received a general briefing on the matter from army headquarters in St. Louis," Tyler said, "but more details would be most helpful. Go ahead."

"Yes sir.

For the next ten minutes Finnegan recounted the circumstances of the robbery. He detailed how Major Brunston and the other thieves fled along the Platte River to a rendezvous point with someone riding a wagon. From there the tracks led across the plains in a westerly direction. When Finnegan had finished, Tyler already had a map spread out on the log.

"Do you have some indication as to where Major Brunston and his accomplices might be hiding?" he asked.

"Yes sir." Finnegan turned to Mosely. "Tell the captain what you know."

"A few times of an evening I've tracked Sioux war parties which come nigh to my place," said Mosely. "They always went north and west. And when I got a few miles out, there were Indian signs everywhere."

"Yes," Tyler said, "but I fail to comprehend what it has to do with the fugitives from the payroll theft."

"I was just gettin to that part," Mosely curtly replied. "Now, any number of times I seen a half-breed named Witt Deaver going past my spread. It's been mostly late of a night. He's always drivin a wagon with..."

"Deaver...Deaver," Tyler interrupted. "That name is quite familiar."

"Yes, Captain, he sells guns to the Indians."

"Of course." Tyler shook his head. "A very dangerous man."

Sighing audibly, Mosely said, "Captain, I know all about Deaver. I've seen him dealin guns to the Indians at least once. So what I'm trying to say is them war parties are goin northwest because they're headin for a powwow with him. So it just makes sense his hideout must be near my place."

"You've got my attention now; keep going."

"Captain, the thing is, Deaver passed my place in his wagon the other day, only he wasn't alone this time. Ridin with him was two men, one wearin an army uniform, and a young woman."

"Aha!" Tyler smacked a fist. "Undoubtedly the fugitives must have made arrangements with Deaver to help them reach the western territories. And so they must be at his hideout right now."

Mosely frowned. "That's it. And, I figure, if this major knows Deaver, then he must be part of the gunrunnin."

"This is an opportunity to kill two birds with one stone," Tyler exclaimed. "We can apprehend Deaver, Major Brunston, his cohorts, and rescue the girl. Quite a coup, if I do say so myself." He turned to Mosely. "Surely you must have some idea how we can locate this hideout?"

"I've been tryin to tell you, I got a notion."

"Excellent." Tyler fairly beamed. "Would this map be useful in explaining this…notion of yours?"

"Possible." Mosely studied the map and found the Platte River.

After several moments of concentration, he tapped a finger on a spot designating a small pond.

"I believe Deaver's holed up nigh to water. And I've ridden round that land and it ain't of much account. Kind of rocky and all full of crags. No good for plantin or grazin. A place folks ain't likely to go. Everythin makes it right for Deaver's hideout."

"I see other areas with water that could serve just as well," the captain said.

"Only trouble bein, they're too far from the Platte and the Missouri, Captain."

"How do you mean, too far?" asked Tyler.

"Well, it's like this," Mosely explained. "As near as I can figure, Deaver does his dealin in the dark at the mouth of the Platte. He drives his wagon over the prairie, meets a flatboat, loads up, and gets back to his hideout afore light. If his hideout was too far out, he'd be caught by now."

"So now we have a rather good fix on our man," Tyler said, studying the map. "We've been riding hard for six days from Fort Kearny. I calculate we're not very far from our rendezvous."

"Rendezvous?" Finnegan questioned. "The one I suggested?"

"I don't know about that," said Tyler, "but we're to meet with a force coming from Fort Randall under the command of Colonel Parkinson. Our agreement is to join them just south of the forested area." He indicated the place on the map. "From there we'll ride to the Platte, then turn east and begin searching along the river in hopes of flushing out the thieves." He paused. "But, of course, all this becomes unnecessary if our little side trip on the way proves to be fruitful."

Finnegan frowned. "No offense, sir, but it looks to me as if you've been playing us all along."

"You're quite right," Tyler replied. "And I apologize for doing so. But I had to know if you were going to tell me anything of substance." He made an attempt at a smile. "It's conceivable that you might have been sent to throw us off in our pursuit of the fugitives."

"I can assure you, sir, we've been telling the truth," said Finnegan. "I forgot, US Marshall Butler deputized me just as I left to go after the payroll."

"That helps," said the colonel, looking at the badge. "But, just to make sure, the three of you will stick with me. Let's go—we've got at least an hour of hard riding."

The four men returned to where Tyler's scout was holding the horses. The group mounted and rode towards the troop column.

Finnegan trotted near Creek and whispered, "How does it look to you?"

"Trouble," he answered. Creek interlocked his fingers. "All the tribes are coming together. They will be many and the soldiers few. And we will be in the middle."

Mosely heard and added a confirming nod. Finnegan sighed and for a brief moment wished he was back on the Mississippi poling a flatboat with his friend, Adas Werrtle.

CHAPTER TWENTY-ONE

Elisha sat and wondered how a major of the army could become so vile and dissolute. She stopped pondering when the sound of horses and wagon wheels came to her ears. Rising, she moved cautiously to her door and peered down the passageway to see Brunston stir from his chair. It had to be Witt returning. How could she warn him? Should she even try? Torn with indecision, she bit her knuckles. She struggled to choose a course of action, time was slipping away. She heard the voices outside and decided she couldn't do anything.

"Not bad, not bad at all," Scower said. "Wouldn't know this place was here in a hundred years. Them rocks and brush back there make a perfect cover."

"Thanks," Deaver replied, reining the horses and wagon to a stop. "Suits me just fine."

"Dug you a house right from the side of a hill, huh?" Scower continued. "Real clever. Yessiree; just like the dog you are."

"Come on, we'll see what Brunston and Winthrup are up to," Deaver said, climbing down from the wagon.

He led the way inside the cave and came to an abrupt halt near the entrance. Brunston leaned against a support beam, pistol in hand. An empty bottle of whiskey lay on the floor at his feet.

"I heard you," said Brunston, displaying a drunken grin. "So you want to know what Winthrup and I have been up to, eh? Well, he's lying dead in the next room."

"Why?" asked Deaver.

"He got a mite over anxious about his share of the payroll and I had to kill him. Lost myself another partner. Now isn't that a shame?" Brunston laughed hoarsely.

"Better put down that gun," Deaver said. "We don't need any more trouble."

"Not quite yet. There's still one last business matter which requires my attention."

"What are you talking about?" asked Deaver.

Brunston jabbed the pistol in the direction of a wide-eyed Scower. "It's nothing personal, Will," he said, "only I don't intend to share that money with anyone."

As the gun leveled and fired, Scower ducked out the doorway and ran toward a horse. Brunston tried to shoulder his way past Deaver. The gunrunner, grabbed Brunston and they fought through the doorway and to the outside. Scower, riding low, raced past them and plunged up the path and out of sight. Deaver, disgusted with the drunken major, shoved him hard.

"Stupid half-baked savage!" Brunston shouted walking back inside the dugout. "You let him get away!"

"He's not going anywhere," said Deaver, following the major. "This is Indian country, remember? Now give me that pistol until you sober up."

"I'll be happy to give it to you," said the major, lifting the revolver, "right through the head."

With one hand Deaver knocked the gun aside. With the other he freed a hunting knife from his belt. He rammed the blade into Brunston's belly then withdrew it and struck again. The second time he let Brunston sag onto the cutting edge before releasing him to the floor.

"You...you've killed me," Brunston mumbled, his face registering astonishment.

Blood flowed from the wound and rapidly pooled on the boards. Gradually the major's eyes glazed over. Only then did Deaver notice Elisha looking on from the passageway, her face pale and frightened.

"I hadn't much choice," he said wiping the knife blade on Brunston's pants' leg.

She didn't respond but walked unsteadily to a chair and sat down. Deaver replaced the knife in its sheath and went into the major's room. Winthrup was sprawled face down across the bed. The blankets beneath him were saturated with blood. A misshapen hole marred the back of his neck where the bullet had emerged. The payroll chest was on the floor at his feet.

Deaver squatted, unfastened and pulled the latch, and lifted the lid to reveal bags of gold and silver. An account statement inside itemized the coins to a total sum of $29,000.00. He opened one bag of newly minted gold coins. It was more money than he had ever seen in his life. Putting the sack back and closing the lid, he carried the heavy box to the main room and set it on a table. He saw the girl sitting as he had left her.

"You'll have to toughen up if you're going to get through this," exclaimed Deaver.

She shook her head, all the while avoiding his gaze.

"I don't mean you any harm. Hope you understand that."

She made no response.

"We'll have to get away from here soon as it's dark," Deaver said. "If that pistol shot didn't raise somebody, then Scower will, rambling around on that horse. And it won't matter much just who it is, Indians or soldiers."

Deaver picked up a bag and began putting air tights in it.

"The Indians want you for a squaw and the soldiers want me for gunrunning. Like it or not, we're stuck with one another. So we might as well get along, savvy?"

Again she made no response, her head bowed.

"Listen, little lady, I had nothing to do with you being here," he said angrily. "And I didn't want to kill Brunston. But what's done is done. Now if we're gonna get out of this alive, you can't just sit there like a stone. Do you hear?"

When she continued to remain silent he grabbed her by the shoulders and shook her.

"Please! Stop!" she cried.

"Got your attention, did I?" he said, squeezing harder.

"I...I heard everything you said."

"You've got no idea what kind of trouble we're in," he said, relaxing his grip. "Out in that rig is a bunch of stolen rifles." He gestured in the direction of the wagon. "If the soldiers find them, I'll hang. Now I'm sure that doesn't mean anything to you. But in the next day or so Hump is coming back here. He wants those guns and he wants you. Do you know what it's like to be a captive?"

"No, and I don't want to."

"Well, it's not very pretty," he said. "Sooner or later they'll start treating their dogs better than you. Then you'll work sunup to sundown, eat what scraps you can get, and hope to die."

Turning her eyes from his, she asked, "What should we do?"

"Once it gets dark we'll set out west along the river. I've got a place there to hide the guns. Then we'll follow the Platte and head north into Wyoming territory."

"And after that?"

"Suit yourself."

"I'll be allowed to go?"

"Yes."

"She thought a moment. "What about the money?"

"It goes with us."

"You mean it goes with you."

"I mean us, so long as you stay put." Deaver went over and retrieved Brunston's pistol. "Can you cook?"

"A little."

"How about seeing to some grub for us while I pack more supplies?"

She nodded and made her way to the stove. He watched her go, then he began dragging Brunston's body into the bedroom with Winthrup's.

CHAPTER TWENTY-TWO

Hump stood just within the circle of light cast by the huge fire. Behind the flames which licked hungrily at the night sky were a number of teepees. Various tribal leaders sat near the fire. Each of them waited to hear the words of the war chief.

"My brothers," Hump began, raising his hand. "We have seen many whites and bluecoats come from the rising of the sun. They have taken our land and killed the buffalo. Now they bring the Iron Horse. They have made many promises, but they do not keep them. Now we wait for our land to be taken, our hunting grounds destroyed, and our way of life ended. Each day more soldiers come to drive us away. I say we have waited long enough, we must act to defend what is ours."

An older chief rose to his feet and lifted his arms. "I would speak now, my brother."

"We will listen, Crying Wolf," declared Hump.

Crying Wolf's eyes were mere slits in the darkened flesh of his face. He stood before the assembly for several moments before commencing to speak.

"It must be remembered the intruders are many," said the older chief. "They have big guns with wheels and many rifles, while we only have a few. More wagons than we can count cross our land. Fire canoes bring soldiers up the great waters to build forts. The Iron Horse is a thing we cannot kill. If we fight against so many, our warriors will die and our teepees will be empty. And still the whites will come."

Crying Wolf looked around with a certain air of dignity before continuing.

"I have lived to see many moons and fought many battles. We must talk to the whites. I have ridden the train to Washington and have seen things I cannot describe. I know they are stronger than we are. Not all men have war in their hearts."

Even as the old chief seated himself, Hump stepped back into the firelight. He carried a Henry repeater in one hand.

"We have strong medicine too, Crying Wolf," he said lifting the rifle overhead. "We will have more rifles, and like the soldiers, we will use guns."

Hump handed the weapon to one of the chiefs. With a sense of awe each of them handled and examined the Henry repeater. Hump waited. It was some time before the rifle was returned.

"Even as we talk, the horse soldiers come from Fort Randall," Hump said. "A great white chief leads them to fight against us. You saw what they did to the Cheyenne leader, Black Kettle. We all know he was the peace chief. See what happened to him and his people. If they wipe out a peaceful village, think what they will do to us!"

A low murmur swept through the ranks of the group.

"We must attack and show the horse soldiers that we are strong," Hump exclaimed. "In one rising of the sun we will hide in the place of the tall trees, and we will kill the bluecoats. We will take their guns, stop the Iron Horse, and save our hunting grounds. We will drive the soldiers and the whites from our land."

A silence came over the entire encampment. There was no sound except a gentle breeze fanning the crackling wood of the fire. Chief Hump stood before them, raised his rifle, and shouted, "Death to the soldiers!"

As Hump finished, several of his followers began shouting, "Death to the soldiers!"

"Death to the soldiers!" Hump shouted.

"Death to the soldiers!" repeated most of the group except for the older chiefs.

The congregation of warriors that stood outside the circle of fire took up the cry, brandishing axes, lances, and bows. Now the drums set to beating, and slowly warriors began to dance.

Smiling ever so imperceptibly, Hump watched the proceedings for a time, then withdrew into the encompassing darkness.

CHAPTER TWENTY-THREE

A warm breeze crossed the plains, bringing with it the muffled sound of hooves. Buffalo were on the move. High above, birds of carrion circled. From a distance, the faint but distinctive whinny of a horse could be heard.

Creek reined up sharply and waited. Several moments passed before his patience reaped reward. He again discerned the faint call of a horse. Kneeing his pony in the ribs, he galloped to where Mosely rode in a crisscross fashion some distance away.

"I hear a horse," he announced quietly.

Mosely asked, "Close?"

"Follow me," said Creek.

They returned to where the scout first heard the sound. Some moments elapsed before they heard it again.

"It's a horse, right enough," Mosely said. "The wind's blowing dead against us from the south and west so it has to be over that way. Could be one of them army scouts."

They proceeded cautiously for less than a quarter of a mile. Now the horse call was very near. Creek and Mosely dismounted and crept forward. The ground dropped away before them into a deep ravine. There Scower crouched, revolver in hand. His eyes were fixed on a prairie dog half out of his hole. A few yards away a horse was picketed.

Rising, Creek called down, "Don't shoot. It will bring Indians."

Scower whirled around, leveling the pistol at his visitor. "Looks like I already done that," he said. "Where'd you come from?"

Creek said nothing.

"Answer me now," Scower demanded, "or I'll kill you sure."

"Settle that hammer easy, friend, or you're a dead man," said Mosely, holding his rifle. "Never you mind turning around. Just do like I tell you."

There was a click of the hammer.

"Real fine," said Mosely. "Now shuck your pistol and we'll do some talkin."

Scower complied, swung around, and glared at the man towering over him.

"What do you want with me?" Scower complained.

"You were on the fire canoe," Creek said. "Maybe you know about the girl."

"Hey, I know you!" exclaimed Scower.

"We're looking for the folks what stole that army payroll," Mosely said. "Tell us where to find them?"

Scower sneered, "I got no idea what you're talking about."

"You don't, huh." Mosely nudged him in the back with the muzzle of his rifle. "Grab those reins and get up that hill."

Creek recovered Scower's pistol and slipped it into his belt. Then the three men and the horse climbed out of the ravine. Finding the other two mounts, they headed back toward the river.

CHAPTER TWENTY-FOUR

Glancing at the sun, Captain Tyler said, "Your friends have been gone for quite awhile, perhaps they've encountered trouble."

"I hope not," said Finnegan.

Just then a corporal rode up and saluted smartly. "Begging your pardon, sir, but the scouts have returned." He pointed out three riders who were approaching some distance off.

"Appears as though they're escorting someone," Tyler said, shading his eyes. "Perhaps it's one of the fugitives."

Finnegan leaned forward in his saddle and peered at the oncoming trio. "Holy Hannah, I can't believe it!" he exclaimed.

"Do you recognize the captive?" Tyler questioned.

"Yes sir. The name is Will Scower. He worked as a steersman on my boat until an injury put him ashore at Fort Leavenworth. Not a few of us suspected he was associated with the payroll thieves."

"How interesting. Then he might prove to be useful."

"I'm afraid you won't find him all that accommodating, sir," Clint commented.

When the three men came to a halt, Scower stared hard at Finnegan but didn't speak.

Captain Tyler turned to his troops. "Company dismount!"

All present followed his orders. The captain turned his attention back to the scouts, and their captive.

"This fella was out yonder attemptin to pot a prairie dog," Mosely said. "Creek claims he was on that steamer carryin the payroll."

"So I understand." Tyler studied Scower closely. "Why are you wandering alone in Indian country?"

Arms folded across his chest, Scower gazed impassively into space as though he had not heard the inquiry.

"Where did you come from?" Tyler persisted.

Still no response.

"You can answer me now," Tyler continued, "or I'll have you taken to Fort Kearny and put in irons. And we'll see how well you survive there, performing manual labor on bread and water."

"I ain't done nothin wrong," Scower protested. "So you got no right to jail me."

"That remains to be seen," said Tyler. "As for your rights, I represent the federal government. You're a suspect in an army payroll theft and will be forcibly detained until the matter is settled. If you cooperate, I am empowered to grant you leniency. Well, what do you say?"

A troubled frown pleated Scower's brow.

"I didn't rob nobody and that's gospel," he responded.

"That's because you didn't get the chance," said Finnegan. "You were laid up in an army hospital."

Scower spit on the ground. "I don't have to answer to you for nothing!"

"Oh, don't you?" Finnegan produced the metal star from his pants pocket. "I'm a deputized federal marshal. Which means I can arrest the likes of you."

"Ain't true," said Scower, evincing surprise.

"It is," Finnegan replied. "Both this badge and my pistol belong to Marshal Hiram Butler. He deputized me before I left the Dakota Dawn. And he told me himself that you had a prison record."

"Like I said, I didn't have nothin to do with any robbery," Scower blurted. "Brunston and Winthrup and three of their men is who done it. Why I..." He halted in mid-sentence, paling noticeably.

"Well, if you weren't in on the theft, how could you know who did it?" asked Finnegan.

"So...so I...I knew about the robbery. That ain't no crime."

"It is if you don't alert the proper authorities beforehand," Tyler said. "You were aboard that boat as an accomplice. Only circumstances beyond your control prevented you from participating in the theft."

Scower slumped dejectedly in his saddle.

"It's obvious the only reason you came here was to meet with Brunston and Winthrup to get your share of the money. We know a man can't be convicted for something he just intended to do. Still, you can receive a stiff prison term for withholding information. Help us and it will go easier for you."

Scower nodded.

"Take us to where Brunston and the others are hiding," Tyler said. "No sense in them getting away with all that money."

His head lowered, Scower considered his predicament.

"Well?" Tyler prodded.

"Don't seem to have a choice, do I?"

"Is the place nearby?" Finnegan asked.

"Four, five miles or so," came the grudging reply.

"How many people are there?"

"Brunston, Winthrup, and a half-breed name of Witt Deaver."

"What about the girl?" Finnegan probed.

"I...I don't know nothin about any female."

Finnegan grabbed Scower by the shirt front. "Don't lie to me."

Scower recoiled. "I ain't lying," he protested. "So help me, I ain't."

"Weren't you at the hideout?" Tyler asked.

"Not really. I didn't get any further than inside the front door."

"Why not?"

"Brunston acted strange and said he killed Winthrup. Then he shot at me and I ran for it. Deaver should still be there with Brunston," Scower explained.

"Shot at you?" Finnegan asked. "How come?"

"I ain't sure. Could of been he was drunk."

Tyler walked some distance away and beckoned for Finnegan to follow.

"Do you think Scower will keep his word?" the captain inquired.

"I'd sooner trust a snake," Finnegan responded. "But the way I see it, we don't have much choice. It might be best if Creek, Mosely and I went with him and you trailed us at a distance. We don't want to tip our hand."

"Good thinking." Tyler checked the sun again. "We haven't much time. I don't want to be late for our rendezvous with Colonel Parkinson's troops. And right now we're about a half hour ride from our meeting point."

"Then we better get moving."

"If there's any problem, just send Creek and we'll come on the run," Tyler said.

"Yes sir."

Mounting up, Finnegan said to Scower, "All right, let's make for the hideout. You ride ahead and we'll stay close behind. If you try anything, you know I won't hesitate to…"

Scower grunted in understanding and slowly turned his horse around. Finnegan motioned to Creek and Mosely and they fell in on either side. Sun-filled plains stretched for miles around with the view unobstructed save for a distant herd of buffalo. Everything seemed tranquil, but Finnegan didn't really believe this would last.

CHAPTER TWENTY-FIVE

Lieutenant Robard rode toward Colonel Parkinson at the head of the column.

"The scouts have returned, sir," Robard said, riding up beside Parkinson.

Parkinson nodded. "Tell Mapes Grunwald to report on the double."

"Yes sir." Robard saluted and, spurring his horse, headed back along the column.

Since sunup no Indian smoke signals had been sighted, a marked departure from the six previous days. It was foolish to think the hostiles no longer had an interest in the detachment's destination. But why weren't there any more smoke signals? Parkinson pondered the possibilities as Grunwald approached. The scout's full beard was tinged with tobacco juice. Perspiration stains heavily marked his shirt and dust clung to his damp forearms.

"Well, Grunwald, what does it look like out there?" Parkinson asked.

"Ain't much stirring, Colonel. Have to say I don't like it at all."

"Did you see any signs of Indian activity?"

"Plenty of pony tracks," Grunwald replied. "War party in size. Nothing real surprising about that except none of them is more than a few hours old."

"What's your point?"

Grunwald spit copiously. "Indians out raiding usually run in kind of a circle. They cover a certain spread of ground, then head back home. When you see different tracks crossing, one set is always older than the other. But that ain't the way it is. What we seen was fresh. What's more, they're heading in the same direction."

"Which is?"

"South and east of here."

"Toward the forested area?"

"Yes sir."

Parkinson looked pensive. "Anything else?"

"I seen more tracks than I like. I'm afraid it's a big war party. Could be Sioux, Cheyenne, Arapaho—maybe all three."

Parkinson rubbed his chin. "So it would seem they're preparing for a united effort?"

"That's my take of it, sir. And a lot of them tracks were deep, which means the riders came a ways carrying extra weight. Food and supplies is my guess."

"Not only a united effort but an extended campaign?"

"Yes sir. Seems like it."

After a interlude of silence, Parkinson asked, "What do you think they have in mind for now?"

"I reckon an attack."

"Us?"

"Yes sir,"

"They'll be waiting somewhere ahead of us?"

"It's what I figure, sir."

"So do I." Parkinson gazed into the distance. "How many do you expect we'll be facing?"

Grunwald stroked his beard briefly before responding. "That's hard to say. From the tracks we seen there could be upwards of a hundred or more. But there's no telling how many of them came from other directions. If I was a betting man, hundreds."

Parkinson sighed audibly. "We can't hope to outrun them. We'll have to pick the most advantageous ground available and make a stand there. Our only hope is that Captain Tyler and his detachment from Fort Kearny arrive in time."

"Yes sir,"

"How much of a ride is it to the forest?"

"Little more than an hour the way we're going."

Shading his eyes, Parkinson glanced at the sun then scanned the land around. "We'll head more to the west and away from the forest. But we'll need to send someone to Captain Tyler and hurry him on his way."

"Want me to give it a run, sir?"

Parkinson smiled. "For a white man to make it would be pretty long odds, wouldn't you think?"

"Yes sir." Grunwald gazed into the distance. "One of our Indian scouts might do it."

"My thought exactly," said the colonel. "Who went with you today?"

"The youngest of the three,"

"Blackbird is his name?"

"Yes sir," said Grunwald. "He was the captured Crow we saved. I trust him."

"Yes, I remember now," said the colonel.

"Want me to get him, sir?"

Parkinson nodded. "And send up Lieutenant Robard on your way to the rear."

"Yes sir."

When Grunwald was gone, Parkinson retreated into his thoughts. Had he needlessly endangered the lives of his men out of concern for his daughter?

CHAPTER TWENTY-SIX

Deaver held a knife against Elisha's side. She was forced to lay behind the scrub bushes, her head resting on the ground. He peered through the leafy branches at the line of soldiers who rode briskly past their hiding place. He remained concealed until he was certain no more of their number were following.

"Those horse troops are looking for something," he muttered as though thinking aloud. "Quite a few of them went by."

"Perhaps they're searching for us," Elisha said sitting erect. "Or at least for that stolen payroll money."

He glared at her. "Well, they're not gonna get it," he said.

"I'm sure Major Brunston and the others felt as determined as you."

"Just what are you saying?" Deaver growled.

"The obvious. You aren't going to escape with it either."

He drew back his hand to slap her and she smirked. "Go ahead and I'll scream."

Lowering his hand Deaver said menacingly, "If I go down, we both go down. Killing won't be a problem for me. Remember that, little lady."

"I thought you didn't intend to harm me?"

"That's right. But only as long as you don't give me any trouble." He fingered the knife in his hand. "You understand?"

"Yes, I do."

"Good." He got to his feet and gazed around him. "Those soldiers trotting up and down are kind of worrisome. So I think we'd better change our plans."

She frowned. "What do you mean?"

"When I'm sure they're gone, we'll head north. Not too far from here is a forest. We can lay over until tomorrow. When it's night again, we'll make for the Niobrara River and take it to the Wyoming territory." Deaver grinned. "There's more than one way to skin a cat."

Elisha turned away, her heart sinking. The presence of soldiers had given her hope. What were the chances of encountering another cavalry unit? None. But what about the Indians? She trembled.

Deaver descended the bank to where the waters of the Platte washed around a rocky projection. The wagon and horses were picketed there, secure from prying eyes in every direction. Reaching under an assortment of skins, he withdrew a parfleche and rummaged through the contents. He extracted a chunk of dried venison and began cutting it into pieces. The meat was salty and tough. He chewed it idly, his thoughts concerned with what lay ahead for him on the morrow.

Crossing the plains alone was a sobering prospect. His gaze drifted to the girl, who stood a short distance away staring into space. She was pretty all right, but strong-willed. Not the kind who would settle for anything other than what she wanted.

And he didn't figure to be the man she had in mind. Probably like pairing a doe with a rattlesnake. The thought made him angry.

I best not get upset. A man with a woman on his mind is a man fixing for trouble. A bad move and I could end up dangling from a rope or rotting in the sun with my scalp missing. If the worst comes, I can use the girl for barter. Hump wants her because she's the colonel's daughter. He grinned to himself. *Might serve the uppity princess right being some chief's squaw.*

CHAPTER TWENTY-SEVEN

Within the forest, Sioux, Cheyenne, and Arapaho warriors huddled in small groups, painting their bodies with colored clay. Some of them ringed the orbit of the eye in dark colors then drew a line from the forehead down the nose to the chin. Others covered their chest and abdomen with jagged marks of various hues while still more formed handprints on their horses. Sacred signs were painted to endow them with extra strength and protection from enemy weapons.

Many of them had counted coup before, as the eagle feathers which adorned their heads verified. Full war bonnets were also in evidence. Warriors carried sheathed knives, tomahawks, and war clubs. Lances, bows, and deerskin quivers filled with arrows lay on the ground. The gunrunner had not appeared as planned, and just a few warriors had single shot rifles. Hump was the only one with a Henry.

All around, ponies were being vigorously walked with the hope they would urinate and therefore be able to run faster. When the last of the preparations had been completed, the shaman, Wolf Dreamer, made his appearance. He wore a wolf skin over his head and performed special rites.

As Hump and other chiefs stood watching, a lone rider entered the wooded preserve, quickly dismounted, and approached. Hump joined him and they spoke privately.

"Are the horse soldiers coming?" Hump inquired.

"Yes, but further west."

"How soon?"

"When the sun makes no shadows," the messenger replied, gesturing straight overhead.

CHAPTER TWENTY-EIGHT

Scower halted and turned his horse. "Deaver's hideout is down there," he said, pointing to the rim of a rocky cliff. "The entrance is hidden between two boulders."

The four men dismounted and tied off their mounts. Creek studied the ground leading to the hideout.

"A wagon came out and headed south," said Creek.

"Can you tell how long ago?" Finnegan asked.

Creek fingered the dirt around the tracks. "Probably last night."

"Question is, who was on board?" said Finnegan.

"Best way to find out is to send our friend for a look see." Mosely motioned toward Scower with his rifle.

"I can get shot going down into that dugout," Scower protested.

Finnegan lifted his Henry. "And you can get shot for not going. What will it be?"

Scower considered the alternatives, then said, "All right, I'll go in. But you've got to cover me."

"Go on," Finnegan ordered. "We'll watch you."

After some hesitation, Scower got on his horse and guided it between the boulders and disappeared.

Finnegan, Creek, and Mosely stood on the hill above the hideout.

"Cozy little place, ain't it?" Mosely remarked. "We can't see a thing."

"Yeah, we better follow close," said Finnegan. "I'll lead."

They untied and mounted their horses. Clint prodded his reluctant mustang down the hill and between the rocks. He followed the path to a dwelling dug out of a hillside. Scower's horse stood in front of the entrance with his head sagging.

"He must have gone inside," Finnegan said as Mosely rode up to join him. "Let's go."

They tied reins to a post and with rifles at the ready they cautiously entered the cave, but saw no sign of Scower. They exchanged puzzled glances while trying to ignore an odor of dead flesh.

"Come out here, Scower," Finnegan said, "while you still got the chance."

Almost immediately Will Scower stepped from an adjoining room, hand covering his nose, and beckoned to them. They came to the doorway of a bedroom and saw Brunston lying dead on the floor while Winthrup was stretched across the bed.

"Got himself knifed," Scower said, indicating Brunston.

Finnegan crouched beside the body and nodded. "A very thorough job too." Then he examined Winthrup's bullet wound. "He was shot from close range."

"This was some fight," Scower said.

"Yes," Finnegan replied. "But we don't necessarily know who was involved."

"Why, them two killed each other," said Scower.

"I don't think so." said Finnegan. "If Winthrup did the job on Brunston, then what happened to the knife?"

Scower frowned and shook his head.

"Look right there." Mosely pointed to a bloody mark on the bedroom floor. They returned to the front room. "Whole lot of blood in here too."

"It appears as though someone pulled Brunston from the front room to the bedroom," Finnegan said.

"Could be Witt Deaver did it," said Scower.

"Must have been him that took off with the wagon," Mosely added. "And the payroll money as well, I'll wager."

Scower muttered something under his breath.

"I bet the lady's gone with Deaver," Mosely surmised.

Finnegan nodded. "I doubt if she went along of her own free will." He thought a moment. "Better send Creek to Captain Tyler. Tell him to ride on, we'll catch up."

"What are you gonna do?" Mosely asked.

"See if I can find anything here that might tell us where Deaver has gone," said Finnegan. "We've got to find the girl."

"I'll go talk to Creek and be back directly," said Mosely.

Mosely went out. When he was lost to view, Scower said, "There's some female things yonder." He gestured toward a connecting passageway.

Even as Finnegan's eyes moved in that direction Scower lunged and knocked the Henry to the floor. He quickly retrieved it and pumped a round into the chamber.

"Now, friend," he said with a grin, "you can just shuck that side arm."

Finnegan hesitated. "And then what?"

"I'm gonna kill you."

"Not smart. Mosely and Creek will hear the shot."

Scower continued to grin. "I already thought about that. I'll just wait, shoot them both first and then you." He motioned with the rifle. "Now do as I say. Get rid of that pistol."

"You kill us and you're alone in Indian country," Finnegan said. "They will have you scalped and stripped before dark."

"I ain't stupid. When night comes I'll make for Omaha and catch me a ride to St. Louis."

"Going to leave without the money?"

Scower's face hardened. "It ain't worth dying over. Now shuck the Colt or so help me I'll..."

"All right, all right," Finnegan replied, reaching for the butt of the gun.

"Go easy."

Finnegan slipped the revolver from the holster on his hip.

"Just toss it in that chair," Scower said.

Frowning, Finnegan swung his arm back slowly as if to do as instructed then threw the pistol at the big man. Scower flinched. Clint rushed at the rifle barrel and grabbed it firmly in both hands. They wrestled for possession, lurching violently about the room. Scower lost his balance against a chair and went down. The abruptness of the fall wrenched the rifle free from Finnegan's grasp.

Scower scrambled to his knees and picked up the Henry. Finnegan dove for his Colt. As Scower took aim, Finnegan rolled, snatched the pistol and scrambled behind some stacked boxes. The rifle barked once, tearing a hole in the board floor. A second blast ripped a corner off one of the boxes.

Finnegan ducked as another loud shot reverberated in close quarters. Scower stiffened and he turned to look at the outside doorway. Mosely stood there, smoking rifle in hand. Scower slowly slumped over backwards.

"I won't embarrass you none by askin how he come by the rifle," Mosely said, eyes twinkling.

Finnegan holstered the revolver and grimaced.

"I wasn't thinking," he replied.

"Could be you was thinkin too much."

"What do you mean?"

Mosely chuckled. "You're right smart on that missing lady, ain't you?"

Finnegan's face colored. "We better catch up to Captain Tyler."

"Gonna leave him with the others?" Mosely gestured to Scower.

"Yes." Finnegan recovered the rifle. "I have to say things worked out just like it says in the Good Book."

"How's that?"

"It's states plainly that the wages of sin is death," Finnegan replied. "And just look around you. Everybody who had a part in the payroll robbery is dead."

They went out and Creek was holding the horses reins. Soon they were trotting across the prairie back towards Captain Tyler's troops.

CHAPTER TWENTY-NINE

Blackbird, the Crow scout, rode low on the back of his pony, keeping to the depressions of the surrounding land. He was constantly aware of the forest which lay just south and west. Buzzards were already circling high above. They seemed to know when death was going to put in an appearance. For miles around the sign of many war parties could be discerned. Earlier Blackbird had tracked them to the woods and knew what their gathering meant. He must get through to the soldiers from Fort Kearny if Colonel Parkinson and his friends were to survive.

Emerging from a thick growth of brush, he saw a wisp of dust several hundred yards off and knew enemy scouts were about. He prodded his horse in the ribs and walked it slowly forward.

Frequent glances behind him failed to reveal any more dust plumes. Gradually he veered to the west in the direction of a small spring which was hidden among a cluster of trees and shrubs. There he'd water his mount and study the surrounding terrain. He hoped the Fort Kearny horse soldiers were nearby.

He entered the enclosure and for several minutes he stood listening and looking. Finally he led his pony to water and let him drink. But when he squatted to satiate his own thirst, his horse suddenly raised its head. Blackbird looked up. Directly across from him stood an Indian in war paint, holding a knife in his hand.

"Again we meet," the Indian said. "You should have died many months ago and not played traitor for the whites."

Blackbird rose, his face expressionless. "You tried to kill me. They saved my life. It was you, Horned Elk, and your tribe that wanted me dead."

"I'll kill you now, Crow dog. Then I'll scalp you."

Making no reply, Blackbird removed a knife from the sheath at his waist and stood ready. When Horned Elk came around the spring he stepped to meet him. They circled one another. Horned Elk made several feints, but Blackbird easily slipped out of reach, being careful not to commit himself. Finally Horned Elk kicked viciously and landed a glancing blow to the side of Blackbird's leg. The kick made contact and it hurt, but he was able to keep his feet.

They closed, each grasping the knife hand of the other, and strained for advantage. Horned Elk managed to hook his leg in behind Blackbird's weakened knee and they went down heavily on the matted grass. As lithe as a cat, Blackbird rolled over. Once more they sparred until Horned Elk clamped Blackbird's knife hand in an iron grip and thrust with his own blade.

Blackbird was able to parry the blow, but the knife's cutting edge sliced through his buckskin shirt and stabbed into his shoulder. Blood gushed forth as they grappled for position. Horned Elk worked an elbow beneath Blackbird's chin then pushed with his full weight in an effort to crush the larynx. The effort left him momentarily off balance and allowed Blackbird to drive a knee into his opponent's groin. Horned Elk grunted and doubled over. Blackbird stabbed his blade into the warrior's neck. Crimson flowed from Horned Elk's artery in a torrent of blood, some spurting into Blackbird's face, and then his adversary fell.

Blackbird sat down, gasping for breath. After a time, he got to all fours and stared numbly at his blood-sodden shoulder. Lightheaded and weak, he grabbed moss and placed it inside his shirt and over the wound.

Rising, Blackbird's only thought was to reach the Fort Kearny soldiers and deliver his message. Taking a deep breath, he staggered to the waiting pony. Still dazed, he fell against it before being able to mount.

The horse began making its way west at a walk. Blackbird clutched its mane to keep from falling. Out on the open plain he tried to maintain a course which would bring him in contact with the approaching horse soldiers.

CHAPTER THIRTY

Riding hard, Mapes Grunwald waved his hat in circle over his head. Immediately the column of cavalry broke for a high hill. The bearded scout followed, choking in the massive shroud of dust which rose in the wake of the cavalry horses. Some distance off, mounted Indians raced across the prairie. They came in two different bands, threatening to engulf the badly outnumbered horse soldiers.

The troopers took up their defensive positions around the crest of the high ground. They quickly stacked saddles and bed rolls, stripped the pack animals of their equipment, and improved the makeshift barrier. The horses were contained in the center of the circle. Some of the soldiers lay prone while others knelt. Every man was sighting down his rifle. Behind them roamed the two officers, Parkinson and Robard, shouting orders.

Sunlight reflected brightly from the painted and perspiring bodies that surged up the face of the hill. Shrill war cries sounded throughout the sweltering atmosphere. The harsh wailing unsettled even the most experienced veterans.

"Pick yourself a feather bonnet," Grunwald told a young recruit beside him. "They're chiefs and honored warriors. We get enough of them the first lick, they'll break off the charge."

Down the line Robard gave his men the same instructions. "Fix on the Indians wearing a headdress," he shouted. "Kill them, and we'll split their ranks."

An experienced sergeant stood facing the oncoming charge and gave orders in short, brief sentences. "Don't waste any ammunition on small targets," he said. "Get your bead right where the rider and horse come together. Hit one or the other. Ain't none of them but flesh and blood, like us."

From his vantage point at the top of the rise, Parkinson scanned the enemy ranks. He watched as they fanned out to surround his temporary emplacement. Even though he had been told by the scout, he couldn't believe such numbers. Close to three hundred armed warriors, he determined. If Captain Tyler's troops didn't arrive soon, they needn't bother at all.

"Fire!" The cry echoed along the rim of the defense, and carbines erupted in deadly union. The rifles belched death into the screaming onslaught. Horses squealed, reared, and bolted, suddenly devoid of riders. Screams of the dying and those lusting for battle mingled in an awful cacophony. Flights of arrows hissed overhead and gunshots continued to blast into the air. The first wave of Indians was badly broken. The second group managed to vault the barrier and bring knives, guns and tomahawks into play at close quarters.

From the rear, the mess sergeant carefully aimed a Colt revolver at an Indian intent upon clubbing a soldier. A few yards away, Robard grappled with a knife-wielding assailant. An enlisted man, his coat soaked with blood, smashed the brave on the head with the stock of his rifle. Then both soldier and Indian fell dead. Scrambling to his feet, Robard turned to another warrior, drew his sword, and drove it into the adversary's chest.

"Hold your fire!" Gunfire diminished and then stopped. The command came to an uneasy silence as the Indians withdrew to the plains below. The war party promptly began to organize. Colonel Parkinson hurried to assess the condition of his men. Moans and muffled voices continued to be heard from Indians in the field and from the group of soldiers on the knoll. This was amplified by a warm breeze.

Parkinson walked rapidly along the defensive line, dispensing words of encouragement and calling for what was left of his men to prepare for the next onslaught.

"Move the dead and wounded behind you," he shouted. "The rest of you draw the barricade in tighter. Make it more difficult for them to penetrate and give less ground for us to defend."

When the colonel had passed by, a corporal leaned close to his sergeant and asked, "Don't lumping together make us a better target?"

The sergeant nodded. "But they ain't missing us now," he replied. "So it's better to keep them off our backs."

"Lot less of them warriors," said one soldier.

"I know, a whole lot less than what they started with," said another.

"And fewer of us," the corporal added.

Once more the sergeant nodded.

"Drink sparingly," Robard commanded the remaining members of his troops. "Just a mouthful at a time. No telling when we'll get fresh water again."

Shaking his head, a soldier muttered to his companion, "Not likely it'll be this side of the everlasting."

"Here they come!" came the cry.

This time the Indians charged in one large group. As before, the warriors suffered heavy losses, running headlong into the muzzles of the troopers' guns. Most of the charging phalanx managed to breach the encampment perimeter. A hand-to-hand battle ensued within close quarters.

Mapes Grunwald calmly shot a lance-wielding warrior through the chest, then narrowly avoided being trampled by his wild-eyed pony. When the Indian horses had vaulted back over the barrier, Grunwald turned to check on a young recruit. He found him lying in a curled up position, a barbed arrow lodged through his neck.

A short distance away, the career sergeant blocked a clubbing blow with his rifle and brought the gun butt around to fell his opponent. The Indian rolled over into a crouch only to have a bullet carve open his brow. He sank to the ground as a second bullet tore into his chest.

Colonel Parkinson fired his pistol at a heavily muscled warrior. The hammer clicked on an empty chamber and the big Indian came at him, wielding a knife. In a desperate attempt to gain respite from the gradually descending blade, Parkinson slipped head and shoulder to one side. The glistening point dropped abruptly and lodged in the officer's bicep. At the last moment he succeeded in throwing the

Indian off balance, freeing his right hand. Teeth clenched, the colonel jerked a spare pistol from his belt and fired twice. The first shot burrowed into the ground but the second struck the Indian in the side. The warrior grunted, his features contorted in rage, and he lunged for the gun. A third shot shattered his face and he died, sprawled across Parkinson's chest.

As suddenly as it had begun, the second attack ended. An eerie quiet came over the battlefield. Robard searched for the colonel, found him, and pulled the Indian's body off his commander's chest.

"You're wounded, sir," he said noticing the colonel's bloody arm.

"Help me sit up," Parkinson rasped.

Lieutenant Cale Robard propped him against a tree trunk and set about binding his wound. Sweat blotched Parkinson's brow and his complexion was gray.

"Lieutenant, I'm going to dispatch you to Captain Tyler," he said.

"But, sir, hasn't a scout been sent already?"

"Yes. Only we have no way of knowing if he got through or not. It's quite possible he was intercepted."

"Perhaps someone else should go, sir. I can be of more help here."

"No, Lieutenant, we're beyond help. We can't hold out much longer."

"Sir, I wouldn't leave you and ..."

"I'm ordering you to go, Lieutenant," Parkinson said, his tone taking on a sharp edge. "You must inform Captain Tyler about the size of the enemy force here. The tribes have come together to defend their land. It is too late, much too late, for negotiations."

"Yes sir." Robard looked crestfallen.

"Listen carefully now; we haven't much time before they'll be coming."

"Yes sir."

"Warn Captain Tyler not to try and intervene on our behalf."

"But, sir ..."

"At ease, Lieutenant. There isn't anything the detachment from Fort Kearny can do. It's simply a matter of numbers."

"Yes sir."

"When you return, see to it that our dead get a proper burial and their families are notified."

"Yes sir."

"Good. Take Mapes Grunwald with you. Disguise yourself. They shouldn't notice you leaving to the west."

Lieutenant Robard stood and saluted.

"Oh, Lieutenant."

"Yes sir?"

"Should you ever have occasion to meet my daughter, tell her I love her very much. In any event, I'll see both of you on the other side..."

His eyes damp, Robard hurried away. When he had passed down the line, the sergeant approached Colonel Parkinson.

"May I speak with you a moment, sir?"

"By all means, Buck. How are you, old friend?"

"Good as some, no worse than others, sir." The sergeant knelt beside his commanding officer. "Just wanted to say how much I enjoyed serving under you, sir."

"Buck, the pleasure was all mine. Believe me." Parkinson grasped the sergeant by the arm. "You were always the best of the best."

"Here they come!" This time the men took their positions with a sense of dread.

"Well, sir, I'll be getting to my post." The sergeant stood at attention and saluted. "Maybe we'll get to do some right smart soldering up top, sir."

"I know we will, Buck. I just know we will."

Alone again, Parkinson rose with effort and leaned heavily against a tree. He picked up his Colt revolver and rested it against his leg.

At the rear of the encampment Lieutenant Robard and Grunwald were hurriedly changing their clothes. The dead Indian's buckskin shirt and leggings were almost a perfect fit. A blessing, Robard thought as he rubbed dirt and grime on his face and hands. Beside him Grunwald was doing the same. Both exchanged their boots for pairs of beaded moccasins. Grunwald appropriated a buffalo hat.

"We better be going, Lieutenant," Grunwald said. "Sure you can ride bareback?"

"That's how I learned as a kid."

Several Indian ponies remained at the top of the hill. Mapes captured bridles of two paints and led them into the brush. Robard followed. As the charge began from below, the two men waited. In a matter of minutes the first Indians jumped the barrier and the fighting commenced in earnest. Mounting up, the lieutenant and the scout took advantage of the melee. Riding low, they leaped their horses over the rear barricade and followed behind a group of mounted warriors.

For several terrible moments they seemed to be trapped in the howling horde. But, resolute, they managed to drift through the Indian band until they reached the open prairie. Emerging from the thick veil of dust, they broke into a full run. Soon they were heading south toward the Platte River. Behind them the crest of the hill was almost completely obscured with smoke and dust of battle.

CHAPTER THIRTY-ONE

Creek warily approached the riderless horse. The animal stood still as the scout drew near and its muscles tensed. Blood was smeared across the neck and blanket of the dusky dun.

Mosely came riding up. "Where'd you find the pony?" He asked.

"Right here," Creek replied, "Looks like the wounded rider fell off." He pointed to blood stains.

Creek and Mosely started back-tracking the path the horse made in the tall grass. Less than a hundred yards away they found a wounded Indian lying face down. Mosely held the Henry repeater at the ready as Creek rolled the young man over.

"He's dressed like an army scout," said Creek.

They draped the Indian over his horse and headed back to the column of soldiers.

"Scouts returning with an extra horse," said Finnegan, pointing across the plains.

"So it seems," Tyler replied.

When the two men reined up, Finnegan asked, "Is he dead?"

"Most near," Mosely responded. "Found him lying yonder. Creek thinks he's an army scout."

Several soldiers came forward, lifted the Indian, and placed him on the ground.

"Find the surgeon," Tyler ordered.

"Looks like a knife wound, and pretty deep," said Finnegan. "He's lost a lot of blood."

"Pale as a ghost," Mosely remarked.

Creek looked closely at the wounded man's horse. "This is an army blanket," he said, pointing to an inscription.

Tyler frowned. "Is it stolen, do you suppose?"

Finnegan knelt and searched the Indian. He felt something under his shirt and pulled out a piece of paper. "What's this?" He glanced briefly at the message. "It's for you, Colonel."

Tyler read it and frowned deeply. "It's from Colonel Parkinson. He says there's a large force of hostiles and he expects to be attacked. He asks us to come at once."

The field surgeon approached and administered to the scout. After the wound was dressed, the doctor poured water from a canteen onto the young Indian's lips. The injured patient became conscious, swallowed, and took notice of the soldiers around him.

"My name is Blackbird, army scout," he said faintly, lifting a hand and pointing to himself.

"Yes," said the colonel leaning closer.

Blackbird gestured weakly. "Scout for Fort Randall. There's a large band of Sioux and other tribes near the woods."

"He's awful weak from loss of blood," the doctor said.

"Blackbird, thank you for bringing the message," said the colonel. "Several of you men carry him to the supply wagon. Do it quickly, we've got to move out right away."

CHAPTER THIRTY-TWO

Still cautious in their escape from the Indian attack, Lieutenant Robard and Grunwald halted their ponies and looked back. A thick spire of smoke rose from where the battle took place. They began to strip away as much Indian clothing as they could.

"I pray the colonel and the rest of them died quickly," Robard said, a look of anguish on his youthful features.

"I do, too," Grunwald replied.

Robard considered their surroundings. "Do you think it's safe to head south?"

"Safe as it's gonna be, I reckon." Grunwald peered at the sun. "If we're to find the Fort Kearny detachment, we'd best be about it."

"All right. You lead."

"We'll keep to low ground," said Grunwald.

"Sure don't want to miss Captain Tyler's troops," Robard said. "I have to deliver Colonel Parkinson's message."

"They'll have scouts out. Probably find us before we find them." Grunwald kneed his horse into a walk. "You best lay back a piece, so we don't raise too much dust."

Robard nodded and they rode south towards the Platte.

CHAPTER THIRTY-THREE

The screams of dying soldiers did not so much as turn Hump's head. Eyes as gray as slate, he stepped over the corpses of both friend and foe. He walked to the charred remains of the soldiers' supplies.

"Where is the soldier chief?" he asked a warrior who was picking up a bluecoat's rifle.

"I do not know."

"Find him," Hump shouted. "I want his hair."

The hillside was teeming with members of the war party. Most of them were collecting weapons and ammunition. But all of them stopped what they were doing at the sound of Hump's voice.

"Search for the soldier chief! Find him!"

A dull murmur could be heard as they began looking among the dead for the fallen colonel. Just then an Indian rode up on a lathered paint and approached Hump.

"Soldiers come!"

"Where?"

The messenger swung his arm to the south and west.

"How far away?"

"Not far and they come fast."

"How many?" asked Hump.

"I could not tell. Too many scouts for me to get close."

Nodding, the Sioux war leader considered his alternatives. *The battle was brief but fierce. The soldiers, though few in numbers, fought bravely—too bravely. So many of my warriors lie wounded and dead. Chances are, we can still defeat the bluecoats. But, do I risk more death? My braves celebrate their victory. Better to wait and fight another day.*

"Take our dead," Hump shouted, "burn what remains. We go now."

Members of the war party took up their fallen, put them on horses, and rode for their village. Remaining warriors threw soldiers' bodies and their equipment onto the fire that burned at the top of the hill. Flames leaped and smoke rose into the sky. Today was good medicine for the Sioux, Cheyenne, and Arapaho.

CHAPTER THIRTY-FOUR

Elisha didn't know how long she had been concealed beneath the foul-smelling cover of animal skins, but it seemed an eternity. The wagon pounded unevenly over the prairie and its motion made her sick to her stomach. She rose on her hands and knees to better observe their location. All around them were rough rolling plains. Some distance beyond the bobbing heads of the horses, loomed a dense stand of trees. No doubt it was the forest land to which they were headed.

While she squinted into the light, indistinct shapes could be seen far off. Deaver reined in hard and the wagon stopped abruptly.

"What's the matter?" she whispered.

"Indians," came the hushed reply. "More Indians than I've ever seen in my life."

Panic overcame her entire being. "What...what are we going to do?"

"Leave that to me. You just get down under those covers and stay there."

Deaver flicked the horses with the reins and they began pulling again. He directed them into a shallow depression and halted. Defying Deaver's orders, Elisha cautiously raised up to get a better view of the situation. A stiff breeze blew and sound traveled easily on the air. The movement of many horses came clearly to them, as did the guttural report of the Indians' voices.

"Are they coming this way?" she asked.

"Don't you mind about that," he snapped. "Just keep out of sight."

"But what if they find us?"

"That's not a concern for me. Only for you."

"I…I don't understand."

"The Indians know me. I sell them guns. As for you, some warrior would give a lot to have himself a pretty white slave. If you don't do as I say, I'll see that he gets one."

"You…you wouldn't sell me?"

Grinning he replied, "Bet on it, woman. Now get under those hides."

Once again she stretched out under the smelly skins. She recalled quite vividly how the big Indian chief had expressed an interest in her. The thought of being taken captive was repulsive. But more sobering was the realization that Deaver would not hesitate to pawn her off to suit his purposes. And for that matter, he probably could find it just as easy to kill her.

She remembered his earlier threat to cut her throat. Now fear dissolved into anger. She was being a fool to lay her hopes for survival on this man. Sooner or later he meant to get rid of her. She pulled back the heavy hide once again. Her eyes focused on the pistol jutting from Deaver's belt. For several moments she simply stared at it. The butt was easily within her reach. Committed to a course of action, she gave no thought to the adverse consequences which might result if her plan failed.

Deaver watched the passing Indians closely. He was attentive to any change in their behavior. He was conscious of movement behind him but paid little heed. Then he felt a sharp tug at his belt and realized his pistol was no longer there. Whirling about, he found himself confronted with the business end of the Colt.

"Give me that gun," he said, a hand slipping toward the knife at his waist.

"Don't do it," she warned. "Believe me, I know how to use this. My father taught me to shoot when I was still a child. And you are no more than another target to me."

He grinned. "You're not gonna shoot me, you little witch, because if you do, those Indians will be all over us."

"That's your concern, not mine," she replied. "You just might throw me to them anyway, so I have nothing to lose by shooting you. And you should also know, I can handle a team and a wagon. I... don't need you...for anything."

"Guess you got me in a corner right enough. Mind my asking what you're gonna do from here?"

"Put you on foot, then I'm heading back to the river and Fort Kearny."

"Better think it over," he said. "Without me you won't last a day out here. You'll get lost and that will be that."

"I'll take my chances. Now get down and start walking."

With extraordinary quickness, Deaver grabbed for her gun hand. The Colt barked and his body jerked with the impact of the bullet. Even as the knife cleared its scabbard, the second shot struck him. This time he went limp, teetering on the driver's seat, then disappeared over the side.

Frightened by the shots, the horses bolted and raced blindly forward. Dropping the gun, Elisha managed to retrieve the reins, but the horses were out of control and refused to slacken their pace. Speeding over uneven ground, a wheel broke and one side of the wagon bounced up into the air. It landed hard, turned over, and she was thrown. The horses broke free, dragging part of the wagon tongue across the prairie.

The hard ground rushed up to meet her. She hit it with neck-rending force, her arms and legs flailing wildly. She came to rest face down, nearly unconscious. Stunned, the last thing she heard and saw were distant voices and painted figures. Then she fell into a pool of inky blackness.

CHAPTER THIRTY-FIVE

It was well past noon and Creek, Finnegan, and Ab Mosely were scouting ahead of the troops from Fort Kearny. They were headed for the rendezvous area. It was Creek who first saw movement. The three scouts dismounted and hid their horses. In the distance, two riders approached on tired mounts. As they came near, Creek stepped in front, rifle at the ready. Mosely and Finnegan came out of the brush, also holding rifles. The two riders held up their hands.

"Who are you?" demanded Mosely.

"I'm Lieutenant Robard from Fort Randall, and this is Grunwald, my scout. I'm afraid our entire command was wiped out."

"Why aren't you wearing your uniform?" asked Finnegan.

"Colonel Parkinson's orders," said Robard.

The lieutenant explained as much as he could. After a few tense moments, Robard was able to convince his captors he was not a deserter. Together, the five men rode back towards Tyler's troops.

"Well?" Tyler inquired as they rode up.

"The Indians attacked and left," Creek replied, gesturing to the east. "These two escaped from the battle."

"That's right, sir," said the mounted soldier. "Lieutenant Robard, sir, and this is Grunwald, my scout. Colonel Parkinson ordered us to disguise ourselves and escape. He wanted us to report to you, sir. He ordered me to tell you that the Indians are organized in mass and to warn you not to attempt rescue. There were nearly three hundred warriors who attacked us and I'm afraid...

Tyler frowned. "You left your command?"

"I know it looks bad, Captain," said Grunwald. "But I was there and heard every word, and this soldier boy is telling the truth. I reckon Colonel Parkinson had his reasons. Didn't want you walking into an ambush."

"Where did this battle take place?" asked Tyler.

"I'll lead you," replied Grunwald. "I'm willing to bet they saw you soldiers coming and they figured to hole up a spell."

"I think the same," said Creek.

"My guess is them Indians ain't going home any time soon," added Grunwald.

Tyler turned. "Why do you say that?"

Grunwald moved in closer. "Those warriors didn't come a long way just to attack a detachment of cavalry. I figure there had to be at least several hundred of em and I reckon more are coming. So it just makes sense they're gathering for a lot bigger reason."

"I agree," said Mosely. "Most of the tracks I saw run deep, meaning they were carrying extra supplies."

Grunwald nodded to Mosely. "I side with what he said. One battle was enough for the day. They're regrouping, perhaps planning to attack one of the forts."

"If there are more coming, good reason for us not to linger in the open like this," Tyler said. "We have neither the numbers nor the firepower to withstand them."

"Have you changed your mind about going to the battle site, Colonel?" Robard asked.

"No, Lieutenant, but I do intend to alter my tactics somewhat," Tyler replied. "Instead of taking the entire unit there, I'll only send a small group of volunteers to report on the situation. Anything larger might invite another attack." He glanced about him. "Any comments?"

"What is meant by a 'small group', sir?" Robard asked.

"Five, six men at the most who will get the job done with haste and return."

"I'd like to be the first to volunteer, sir."

Tyler nodded. "Since you were involved, I had intended you would be the ranking officer, Lieutenant."

"Thank you, sir. And if I might make some suggestions as to the other volunteers?"

"Go ahead," said Tyler.

"I'm asking Mapes Grunwald for obvious reasons, Mr. Finnegan and his companions, and Mosely and Creek. I feel we would comprise a capable group and avoid diluting the strength of your command, sir." He gestured to the nominees. "May I call upon you, gentlemen?"

"I have no objection," Finnegan replied.

Mosely and Creek nodded their assent, as did Grunwald.

"Thank you, gentlemen," said Tyler. "When you return I expect a thorough report."

"Best we get right to it." Mosely said, with an eye to the sun.

"Sergeant!" Captain Tyler ordered. "Be sure to give these men extra ammunition. And find a jacket for the lieutenant, and an army horse."

The sergeant rode off to comply with the colonel's orders.

Robard stared back toward the forested area. "Captain Tyler, sir, I want you to know that I admired my commanding officer very much."

"There isn't any officer of my acquaintance who didn't respect Colonel Parkinson," Tyler said. "His record speaks for itself."

"Yes sir. And thank you."

"I'll be moving the detachment to a hill back yonder," Tyler said. "We'll dig in and wait. We'll have some Indian scouts of our own out watching your progress. God speed."

The sergeant returned with a horse loaded down with supplies, including several shovels. Lieutenant Robard was brought the military jacket and an army mount.

Grunwald, Finnegan, Mosely, and Lieutenant Robard headed out. Creek followed, leading the supply horse. After a hard ride, Grunwald led them to the sight of the conflict.

A smoky haze enveloped the rise where the battle had taken place. Buzzards circled overhead, some dropped and landed next to other carrion eaters which were already on the ground.

"Grunwald, check it out," Robard ordered, his gaze fixed on the hill.

The scout moved forward briskly. Robard led Finnegan and Mosely forward. Clint looked at the ground, which indicated a great number of horses. He tried to imagine how it must have seemed to the soldiers who occupied the high ground. Surely they knew they had no chance for survival.

As they proceeded up the incline, they saw nothing suspicious. Perspiration bathed Finnegan's face and the palms of his hands. It was a nervous sweat. He felt uneasy about what they would find at the top. The encampment at the crest of the hill was a gruesome site. Finnegan saw a hand, covered with grime and dried blood, protruding from the charred remains of two ammunition boxes. The horses stepped over what was left of the homemade barrier and promptly halted. No one spoke a word for several minutes. They could only stare in disbelief. Buzzards were everywhere, clawing and tearing at the burnt bodies heaped in the center of the encampment.

"Blasted birds," Robard roared, drawing a pistol from his hip holster.

Grunwald stayed his hand.

"If the Indians hear us shooting, we'll be just as these poor fellas," he said.

Robard holstered his weapon, hiding tears. "Can't...we stop them?"

Without replying, Grunwald and Mosely dismounted and began to club at the birds with the stocks of their rifles. Finnegan did the same. Squawking hideously, the carnivorous menagerie grudgingly took wing. Robard got down from his horse and walked as though in a trance to the burned pile of supplies and soldiers. He bent low, examining bodies and sometimes moving them aside. He kept at the task in an effort to find Colonel Parkinson. After a time he stood erect, his face drenched in sweat and his hands blackened with gore.

Grunwald eased toward him to offer comfort; then, thinking better of it, withdrew his hand. He turned abruptly and went over to where Finnegan and Mosely waited.

"Most of them is scalped," said Mosely quietly. "Lot of braves must have counted coup."

Finnegan thought about Elisha and the way she had argued with Brunston that night on the Dakota Dawn. She said he was too dramatic about the danger the Indians presented. Back then, he had hoped she was right. She wasn't. There was a price for killing the buffalo and taking Indian land. The tribes would fight for what was theirs. He felt sick to his stomach but was determined not to show it.

"Good thing we came this soon," Mosely said. "Another day or so and the stink would be something fierce."

Robard approached, his eyes continuing to survey the area. "I don't see Colonel Parkinson's body," he said. "Help me search."

They fanned out, scrutinizing the dead. Some minutes later Finnegan inquired, "Where's Creek?"

"Down yonder," Mosely replied, pointing to where the scout stood with his horse at the foot of the hill.

"Something the matter?"

Mosely nodded. "He just don't want to be bothered by any wandering spirits."

"Brunston said he was a baptized Christian," Finnegan said.

"Don't doubt it none," Mosely replied. "But it's hard to shake the ways of one's upbringin."

Grunwald began waving his arms. Everyone but Creek ran toward him.

"See right there. Ain't that the colonel's boot and spur?" Grunwald inquired of Robard.

"I...I believe you're right," Robard dropped to all fours for a closer look. "Those spurs look familiar."

The boot was covered by a piece of canvas from a bedroll. Over the top of it was spread a collection of saddles and other debris.

"He must have gotten buried somehow," Grunwald said.

Finnegan frowned. "It's almost as if somebody set up the whole thing."

"Why do you say that?" Robard asked.

"See how the saddles are spread out," Finnegan said, "so the canvas couldn't blow over?"

"You're suggesting this was done deliberately?" Robard questioned.

"That's the way it strikes me." Finnegan began tossing the items aside. "Let's move the canvas."

Parkinson lay on his side, his hat serving as a pillow. Finnegan knelt down and ran his hand across the colonel's forehead. It was damp.

"He might still be alive," Finnegan said. "Get some water."

Robard unfastened his canteen and gave it to Finnegan. Clint let the warm fluid dribble onto Parkinson's lips. They moved almost imperceptibly.

"Good Lord, he is alive!" Robard exclaimed.

"Just barely," Finnegan said. "He's got a wound in his left arm and the bandage is pretty bloody."

"It's deep," Robard said. "I know, because I wrapped it."

Finnegan grimaced. "The problem now is how to move him."

"We'll have to send someone back for one of the wagons," Robard said. "I'll stay with the colonel and someone can return to the detachment."

"Send Creek," Finnegan suggested. "The rest of us will stay and start digging graves."

"Creek," said the lieutenant, calling below. The scout came up the hill. "I'll write a message for you. Since we don't see any Indians about, I'm asking Captain Tyler to not only send a wagon and his surgeon, but also a burial detail. We can't leave these bodies out in the open."

Lieutenant Robard hurriedly wrote a message and handed it to Creek.

When Creek was gone, Finnegan said, "The odds are against the colonel making it back to Fort Kearny."

"I bet he'll make it." Robard said and watched the Indian scout disappear over the crest of the hill. "He's got to make it."

The sun was setting when they started down the rise to rejoin Tyler's troops. Grunwald took the lead and Finnegan was trailing behind the small detachment. Lieutenant Robard and the surgeon sat beside Colonel Parkinson in the back of the supply wagon. Their horses were tethered to the tailgate. The burial detail of ten men rode in the middle of the column. Mosely and Creek were riding on the flanks.

Finnegan was glad to leave the place of death—leaving it only in a physical sense, because what he had witnessed there would stay with him a long time. He turned in his saddle for a final look and saw the hill dark once again with the birds of carrion. But this time, the dead men were buried many feet below ground. Facing forward, his thoughts drifted to Elisha and he wondered if she was still alive.

As they neared a spring, Creek came back alone.

"We found a wagon," he said to Finnegan. "Come and see."

Robard frowned. "What wagon?"

"Mosley said it belonged to Deaver," Creek explained.

"Deaver? Who's Deaver?" asked Robard climbing down from the colonel's conveyance.

"He's the gunrunner who stole the payroll money and we think he took Colonel Parkinson's daughter," answered Finnegan.

"Just how far off is this wagon?" asked the lieutenant.

"Not far," Creek replied.

"Did Mosely stay with the wagon?" Finnegan asked.

Creek nodded.

"I better take a look, Lieutenant," said Finnegan.

"Then we'll have to split up," said Robard. "I have to get Parkinson to safety. Good luck finding the girl and the money."

Finnegan and Creek rode south for several minutes before Mosely could be seen standing next to an overturned wagon. As they reined in, Mosely said, "The horses broke loose and ran."

Finnegan jumped down and examined the wagon. "It must have been going pretty fast," he observed. "Where did it come from?"

Creek pointed to the south.

"Let's backtrack a ways," Finnegan said, mounting up.

They followed the rut marks made by the heavy wheels. Several hundred yards distant, they came upon a scattering of hides and skins.

"Has to be where the wagon turned over." Finnegan said. "What do you suppose caused it?"

"Must have hit a rock or run into a ditch," Mosely speculated. "But the ground through here don't seem too uneven."

"Something there," Creek said, pointing out an object reflecting in the fading sunlight.

Finnegan dismounted and turned over the metal box. A length of twisted wire held the latch shut. He removed it and opened the lid. Creek and Mosely peered over his shoulder. Inside were bags of gold and silver along with the paper tally.

"Got to be the stolen payroll money," Finnegan said. "It must have been thrown out when the wagon overturned," He closed and secured the lid.

"Wonder what happened to Deaver?" Mosely asked. "Don't seem like he'd just go off and leave the money."

"Maybe he didn't have a choice," said Finnegan. "I'm going to go back a little further."

"Here," said Creek, dismounting and examining the ground. "There were many unshod horses. Someone lay here and is now gone."

Finnegan and Creek continued on foot and shortly came to a body of a man sprawled on the grass.

"Anybody know him?" asked Finnegan .

"Witt Deaver," Mosely replied, getting down off his horse and looking at the body. "Got himself shot right proper. The one in the chest sent him to judgment. One in the shoulder don't amount to much. Whoever done it was up close."

"How do you know that?" asked Finnegan.

"Blast marks on his shirt. Ain't likely he'd let an Indian get that close. Must have been somebody he knew."

"Elisha Parkinson," Finnegan said.

Mosely nodded. "Have to say she crossed my mind, too."

"But why?" asked Finnegan.

"No telling why she done it," Mosely replied. "But Indians must have come onto her when the wagon went bust. It's the only thing that makes any sense."

Finnegan squinted into the distance. "As soon as we get the money to Tyler, I'm going after her."

"All the sign we seen is real fresh," Mosely said. "Bet those tracks will lead back to their camp. I figure them Indians is holed up close by."

"What should we do with Deaver?" Finnegan asked.

"There ain't a shovel among us," Mosely replied. "But anyway, it don't seem right he should fare a whit better than them soldiers did. In part, they're dead because of his gunrunning. So I say, let the buzzards tend to him."

"Harsh, but we don't have time," Finnegan said. "Let's gather the payroll and get back to the troops."

—∞—

"Quite sure you won't change your mind?"

"Yes sir," Finnegan replied.

With a sigh of resignation, Captain Tyler said, "All right, young man, it's your decision to make."

"Yes sir."

"I admire your dedication. It's a long chance trying to rescue Colonel Parkinson's daughter by yourself."

"Couldn't live with myself if I didn't try, sir."

Tyler turned away. "Lieutenant Robard!"

"Yes sir."

"When we get back to Fort Kearny, you can make your report. We want to be on our way as quickly as possible."

"Yes sir."

—∞—

Finnegan sat on a rock beside the spring and watched as the cavalry soldiers readied themselves for their return to Fort Kearny. Maybe it was foolishness on his part, he thought. He didn't want to die. There was so much he wanted to see and do in this life. He had never been happier than those precious hours spent steering the Dakota Dawn up the Missouri River. 'Master pilot' and 'captain' were titles to which he ardently aspired. And now he was so far away from the sounds, the smells, and the swift movement of the water on the river that it almost seemed as though those things had never been part of his life.

And what did he really know of Elisha Parkinson? He had only the fleeting glimpse of her on the boat. Yes, she was pretty and a little more than spoiled. Did he love her? How could he be sure of that? But did it really matter at this point? She was a human being and faced with a life that well might be worse than death. If he could do something—anything—for her, then he would. His heart said to go ahead. And that's all there was to it.

The sound of troops mounting their horses jolted Finnegan from his troubled reverie. He stood to watch the soldiers leave. Captain C.L. Tyler, commander of Fort Kearny, rode to the head of his column, pulled his saber, raised it high in the air, and cut forward and down. The mounted soldiers commenced riding in columns of two.

Lieutenant Robard left the line of march and rode over to Finnegan.

"I appreciate what you're going to do," he said. "And given the same circumstances, I hope I would have the courage to do the same. The good Lord keep you."

With that Robard saluted and galloped off to catch the fast-withdrawing column. After the soldiers were lost to view, Finnegan turned to see Ab Mosely and Creek standing beside their horses.

"Why are you two still here?" he asked.

"We figured a young pup like you needed some help," said Mosely.

Finnegan looked to Creek, who merely nodded in agreement.

"The two of you are as crazy as me," Finnegan said. "Probably end up getting ourselves killed."

"Reckon so," said Mosely. "If we're gonna read any sign, we best get to it."

So saying, he and Creek mounted up and headed out. Finnegan gazed after the two men and then, abruptly coming to his senses, bolted for his horse and hurried to join them.

Creek was determined that the horse tracks at the site of the overturned wagon were those of the Indians who had taken Elisha. For half an hour they followed them. They led to a small lake and a large Indian encampment. The rugged terrain afforded the three men cover. They were safely able to observe the nearby village without being detected.

From their vantage point on a ridge they could see all of the camp. Tepees arranged in a large circle were situated around an open area that bristled with activity. Logs and branches were being piled up by a number of Indian women. War parties of varying sizes kept arriving. The warriors followed a tortuous path which led down from the plain above.

Finnegan and Mosely lay on their stomachs amid a stand of shrubs. Creek stayed back in the brush, hiding the horses.

"Looks like they're getting ready for a celebration," Finnegan whispered.

"Figures to be a big powwow of some kind," Mosely said. "Lots of bonnets around."

"If she's here, where do you suppose they'd keep her?"

Mosely considered the arrangement of the village. "My guess would be that big teepee right twixt of things. It's fit for a chief."

"I see," said Finnegan. "It'll be real tough to reach the lodge without being seen."

"Maybe we best let Creek study things. I'll ask him."

Both men watched the young Indian use cover to descend to the village. A good half hour passed before he returned.

Creek appeared silently before them. He pointed to the proceedings below and then to the large lodge. "The chiefs are here to talk war," he said, "and make other medicine."

"How do you know that?" Finnegan asked.

"I heard them speak," he replied.

"What did they say?"

"They plan to fight against the forts and the Iron Horse, to stop it from running over their hunting grounds."

"Anything else?"

"Chiefs come to honor Hump for winning a battle against the army."

"Where's the girl?" whispered Finnegan.

"She's held in the chief's teepee."

"Why didn't you say that in the first place?" Finnegan looked to Creek. "How do we get her back?"

"When the fire burns high, the warriors will dance and celebrate. Perhaps then."

—∞—

The sun had been down for more than an hour and a great fire burned in front of the meeting lodge. Since dusk, no more war parties had arrived. Creek scouted and learned that only one sentry was posted at the path leading to the village.

"What will you do about the sentry?" Finnegan asked.

"Me and Creek are going down there and fetch him back," said Mosely.

The big man and the scout slipped through the trees. From the hill Finnegan waited and watched.

Warriors could be seen gathering in the light of the fire. Momentarily the drums began to beat and braves started to move and dance in a circle. On every side, the women and children edged forward to view the spectacle. Chiefs emerged from the great lodge and stood just beyond the roaring flames. Each of them wore an elaborately beaded buckskin shirt and leggings.

After long minutes had passed, Finnegan briefly caught a glimpse of Mosely and Creek. The drums continued to beat a steady hypnotic rhythm. Another half hour went by before Clint's companions appeared, carrying the body of a dead sentry. Working feverishly, they stripped the Indian of his clothes and Creek put them on, including a blanket.

Mosely dragged the body into a clump of brush and returned. Clint and the big Indian fighter watched the scout depart.

Creek took care to remain outside the jagged edge of light cast by the fire. He moved at a measured pace behind the crowd of onlookers. Upon reaching the back of the large teepee, he paused for a final look. Satisfied, he bent down and made a quick cut of the buffalo hide, lifted it, and slipped inside. Elisha sat on a reed mat, hands tied to a pole behind her. A single brave stood guard outside the front entrance.

Creek slid forward and tapped the girl's shoulder. She turned sharply in the flickering light. Elisha's eyes were big and round and Creek held his fingers to his lips. He cut the bindings and motioned for her to follow. The young woman, full of fear, shook her head.

Creek leaned forward and whispered, "Fire Canoe Finnegan sends me. Don't yell. I will take you to him. Do you understand?"

Elisha nodded.

"Where is Clint?" she whispered.

"No time to talk. Come."

Near the fire pit was a pile of blankets. He picked one up and held it out. She took it and wrapped it around herself. Creek lifted the buffalo hide and gently prodded her to crawl outside. He followed, and together they quickly rose to their feet. Arranging the blanket over the woman's head, he led her away. They walked behind the Indian gathering and past the empty teepees. Coming to the unguarded path, Creek took the girl's hand and pulled her up the steep incline. They hurried through the brush to the top of the hill where Finnegan and Mosely lay hidden.

"Clint," she said, hugging him tightly. "Is…it really you?"

"Yes, Elisha, come on. We've got to get out of here."

Even as they made their way to the horses, the drum beating stopped. Shouting and whooping could be heard. Finnegan mounted up behind Elisha. Creek and Mosely were already in the saddle. They sprinted across the prairie due east. After a brisk run, they veered south and Creek stopped briefly to cover their tracks. The sky was still dark when they reached Deaver's hideout. Creek dismounted and started through the brush and boulders. The others followed and the scout led them to the dugout.

"I'll ride for help now," said Creek. "I'll try to catch up to the soldiers."

"I hate this place," Elisha said, holding Finnegan's arm.

"Afraid we haven't much choice," he replied. "Creek told me we could never outrun them. He brought us here to hide until it's dark again."

"Do you think they can find us?" she asked, a quaver in her voice.

"We tried our best to hide our trail," Mosely said. "I figure they won't be searchin for you long. They want to kill soldiers more than find you."

"I...I'd rather die than be captured again," she shuddered.

"Let's hope it doesn't come to that," Mosely said gazing at the dugout. "I kind of wonder if them dead fellas in there has got to really stinkin by now. Guess I better go see."

Finnegan and Elisha stood some distance from the dugout.

Clint watched the girl closely. "You all right?"

"Absolutely not. But I'm much better with you."

Without thinking, Finnegan took her in his arms and held her close. There was no resistance.

Mosely reappeared in the door of the dugout. "Those fellas are smellin bad and we can't use the place. On the way through, I grabbed some stores to feed ourselves."

"What do we do?" asked Finnegan.

Mosely set the bag of supplies down. "I reckon we'll sleep outside." He sized up the situation between the two young people. "I see I ain't wanted here right now. Guess I'll go unsaddle and hobble the horses."

"You took an awful chance tonight," Elisha said, gazing into Clint's face. "Why?"

"It was the right thing to do. Besides, it was Creek who rescued you."

"And that's all there is to it?" she asked.

"Isn't that a question you know the answer to before you ask it?"

"I think so," she said. "But I'd still like to hear it."

"The truth is, I did it because I care about you."

She smiled and looked up at him. .

As the shadows of the evening darkened, their lips met in a prolonged kiss. Together they walked arm-in-arm toward where Mosely was setting up a lean-to and bedroll for the girl. Elisha stepped away, arms folded across her chest, and stood in a contemplative pose. Tears brimmed her eyes. Finnegan placed a hand on her shoulder. He began talking to her about her father and told her everything.

"I thought it best to explain just what happened," he said. "He's had the hand of God on him."

She nodded, her lips set in a rigid line. He could see she was quite determined not to cry.

"Want to be left alone for a while?" he asked.

"No, I don't want to be alone at all," she replied. "Thank you for telling me about my father. Poor Papa!"

"Your father is a brave man, a tough man," Finnegan said. "I have a strong feeling he'll survive and the two of you will be together again."

Mosely stepped closer. "I set up a bed and shelter for the lady. Finnegan, you can fix a supper of cold beans. I'll stand watch up top. I'll tell you when to relieve me."

Mosely and Finnegan took turns standing guard through the night. Just before daylight Clint fixed another meal of beans. After handing Elisha her food, Finnegan carried a portion to Mosley, who was still on watch. Then Finnegan fed and watered the horses.

Mosely came rushing forward, rifle in hand. "We got callers. Looks to be a Sioux war party."

"Dear God, no," Elisha rasped.

Finnegan pulled her back behind the lean-to. "Just stay here and don't come out for any reason."

"Do you think Creek reached the soldiers?" asked Finnegan.

"Could be," said Mosely. "But it's gonna be a good while before we see troops."

"Think we can hold them off until then?"

Mosely made a wry face. "Not a chance."

Up above, Indians on horseback lined the rim of the sheer wall which enclosed the hideout. Finnegan retrieved his rifle from where it leaned. Mosely went over to his saddlebags and collected all the cartridge containers for the Henry's. When he returned to Finnegan, a commanding voice called down to them.

"Hear me, whites. It is Hump who speaks to you. I have come for the woman. I want her alive. You give her to me and we will go. If not, you die."

"She's staying right here," Finnegan shouted.

"You keep her?"

"That's right," yelled Finnegan, waving his rifle.

From above, they overheard a brief but animated conversation between the Indians. Hump appeared once again on the rim.

"I will offer you a fair chance. You will fight one of my warriors," he said. "The winner takes the woman. What do you say?"

"Don't do it, Clint," Elisha called out from behind the lean-to. "Don't do it; you'll be killed."

Clint nodded to Mosely. "This is something I know how to do. Just keep me covered."

"Do you agree, white? Will you fight?" Hump shouted.

"I agree," Finnegan called out. "Send down your man." Clint put aside his rifle and slipped off his holster and pistol. Mosely handed him his hunting knife.

"Watch out, boy," Mosely warned. "They're brought up learnin to fight. That brave will try every trick."

"I have no doubt he will. Could be, I'll teach him a few new ones."

Finnegan stepped out into the open and waited. A very tall and muscular Indian came down the trail on foot. Clint watched him move silently forward.

"He's a Minneconjou Sioux," said Mosely.

What the warrior saw was a big red-headed man, nearly as tall and well-built as himself. The icy blue eyes of the white appeared unafraid. The Sioux had fought such white men before and knew this fight could go either way. Unusual for him, the brave questioned whether his medicine would be good enough.

Finnegan held his knife tightly in his right hand. "We're going to settle this like they do on the docks in New Orleans—winner take all."

The Indian's eyes narrowed as he came forward. "Fight, white man."

"Oh, I will."

Without comment, the brave ran towards Finnegan. The Indian's biceps rippled as he made a wide sweeping slice at his opponent's chest. Finnegan slipped to the side and the knife's thrust missed him. Both fighters circled, crouching low, knives held before them.

"Are you ready?" goaded Finnegan.

The Indian grinned, then suddenly tried to jam the fingers of his left hand into Finnegan's eyes. But a thick forearm swept aside the Indian's darting hand. Both stabbed with their knives and the blades clashed loudly. Clint, with his left fist, struck out with a short punching blow. It slammed into the brave's face. It was a meaty sound. Stepping back, the river man saw a twisted nose leaking blood. The

Indian fighter staggered backwards only to receive a vicious kick to his chest that sent him sprawling. He dropped his knife and Clint kicked it away.

"Now, it's back to scratch," shouted Finnegan, intimidating his adversary. "You don't want to look bad in front of your people."

Eyes bleary with pain, the warrior spit out a mouthful of blood and pushed himself to a standing position. He swayed uncertainly for a few seconds. His short, shallow breathing indicated broken ribs.

They crouched opposite one another, hands suspended.

This time the warrior leapt high and kicked Finnegan backwards and snatched up his fallen knife. Both advanced, and each caught the knife hand of the other in powerful grasps. They struggled, tripped, and went down together. Landing on his back, Finnegan thrust his forehead against the Indian's shattered nose. Finnegan quickly slipped to one side and deftly came to his feet. Then he threw himself down heavily on his opponent's damaged ribs.

"I'm just about done with you," Finnegan shouted, throwing his own knife towards Mosely.

Clint got to his feet and pulled the warrior erect, only to level him with an overhand right to the chin. The battered brave dropped as if felled with an ax and lay motionless, his hand still in possession of his knife.

"Kill him!" a voice demanded from the rim of the wall.

"You kill him," Finnegan responded.

Then he wrenched the knife from the brave's hand and walked slowly away. When he neared his friend, Mosely, a shot rang in the air. Looking up, he saw Hump holding a smoking rifle.

"You fought fairly and spared my warrior's life. I will keep my word. Take the woman and go. But I tell you this, white man—leave our lands, or next time you die."

"Why did they do that?" Finnegan asked.

"Complicated," Mosely replied. "You showed honor and didn't kill. Like he said, next time we won't be so lucky."

They watched as two members of the Sioux war party came down and picked up the injured warrior. They carried him up the hill. Hoofbeats could be heard retreating into the distance.

"We best be getting out of here," Mosely said, throwing his saddlebags over the neck of his paint.

When there was no response, he glanced over to see Finnegan and Elisha in each other's arms, unmindful of his presence. He shook his head and went to gather the other horses.

CHAPTER THIRTY-SIX

With an attentive eye, Finnegan studied every eddy and vortex in the waters through which the blunt bow of the Dakota Dawn plowed. Each of the whirlpools spoke of hidden snags and sandbars that could ground a boat or rip its bottom to shreds. Instinctively, his hands worked the wheel so that the steamer forged a foaming path away and around these submerged terrors. Late rains had bloated the Missouri River, making its passage not so treacherous as it would be in the dryer months of late summer.

Only a few minutes ahead was the landing at Fort Randall. It was a name that stirred many remembrances of events so recently concluded. Just then, the wheelhouse door behind him opened.

"I'll take over now, Mr. Finnegan."

"All right, sir."

Glazer situated himself at the wheel, eyes fixed on the river. "Have you talked to Lieutenant Harbaugh as yet?" he inquired.

"Yes sir. We had a few words when he came aboard."

"That young man is very blessed to be alive."

"He is indeed, sir."

"After these horse soldiers get off at Fort Randall, we'll be taking on more cargo for the run to Yellowstone. You might see if there's enough wood to keep going."

"Yes sir."

Closing the wheelhouse door behind him, Finnegan descended to the main deck where a collection of cavalry officers were standing at the rail. Before them the non-commissioned soldiers were waiting to disembark. Their bed rolls and other gear were slung over their shoulders. Finnegan heard someone call out to him. Turning, he saw Lieutenant Harbaugh approaching.

"I'm leaving," he said smiling, "and wanted to say good-bye. Don't know when we might run across one another again."

"No telling, that's for sure." Finnegan grasped the outstretched hand.

"As I mentioned earlier, I'm grateful for all you did for me out there on the Platte," said Harbaugh.

"Most of the credit goes to Abner Mosely's Indian friend," Finnegan replied. "She nursed you past the pearly gates."

"That's the truth," said Harbaugh. "Tell me, have you and Elisha set a wedding date?"

"No," Finnegan answered. "We decided to let the subject rest awhile. Right now she wants to make certain her father has everything he needs for a full recovery. And I've got a lot to do and learn, to get my captain's license."

"I see."

The whistle on the roof of the wheelhouse blew loudly as the boat began to move toward the landing.

"Did you ever hear how Colonel Parkinson survived the massacre?" Harbaugh asked.

Finnegan nodded. "One of his men hid him under a canvas cover. To my mind, that's devotion above and beyond the call."

"Did anyone figure out who it was?"

"Not really," Finnegan replied.

"That's unfortunate."

"Perhaps, but the good Lord knows; and that's the tribunal in which one wants to hold favor."

"Amen to that," Harbaugh added.

While they talked, the Dakota Dawn was made fast to the wharf.

"Think you'll like Fort Randall?" Finnegan asked.

Harbaugh shrugged. "It'll be full of ghosts," he replied. "The massacre will have a profound effect on the place for some time. And well it should." He gazed into the distance. "Before this is over, there will be a lot of senseless killing on both sides. But, right or wrong, the west will be conquered. At what price, I don't know."

The gangplank was put in place and an order followed, "Troops, prepare to depart!"

"Well, all the best, Clint."

"Same to you, Lieutenant."

Finnegan went to oversee the unloading. When the soldiers reached the dock, they were marched off to the fort. The entire process required only a matter of minutes. Immediately, crew members began bringing the new cargo aboard.

Once assured the loading was under control, Finnegan called for Duke. The big dog bounded to his heels and together they went off to seek additional fuel for the boilers. No sooner had his feet touched the landing than a heavy hand halted him.

"Be needin any timber for that right handsome steamer, river man?" a familiar voice questioned.

Whirling about, Finnegan found himself confronting Mosely, a toothy grin evident in the great bush of his beard.

"Holy Hannah, what are you doing here, Ab?"

"I took to wood hawkin," Mosely explained. "Gonna make me a fortune, then go lay up in style." He laughed at his own humor.

"What happened to your place over on the Platte and Pacho?"

Mosely tapped a thick finger to his brow. "The army took my place for an outpost and gave me a pocket full of greenbacks along with a job scoutin here at the fort. So in between, I got me a wood yard and a couple of partners. And Pacho came with me."

Finnegan looked around. "Where's the wood?"

"Up yonder." Mosely indicated a cabin sitting among a stand of trees on a hillside. "Come on, I'll show you."

As they approached, Finnegan could see two men cording and stacking wood.

"Guess who's here!" Mosely called out.

When he walked up to the men, Finnegan let out a whoop of recognition.

"How are you doing, Fire Canoe?" said Creek.

Finnegan took hold of Creek's forearm and they shook arm and hand for a long moment. Blackbird remained stiff and resolute some distance from the two men.

"You know Finnegan," Creek said, beckoning to the young Crow.

They also shook arm and hand. "Glad to see you're faring better," Finnegan said.

Blackbird grinned. "I'm feeling good, Mr. Finnegan."

"Now then," Mosely said, rubbing his huge hands together, "won't you be needin some wood for them hungry boilers on that boat of yours?"

"What do you have?"

Mosely, with an air of pride, gestured toward three tall stacks of chopped wood. "Over ten cords there."

"I'll take the lot of it," Finnegan said. "Get it aboard and I promise you better than the going rate."

They set to work and he walked slowly to a point on the bank where the Dakota Dawn could be seen riding easily beside the landing. There he knelt down, putting an arm around Duke and getting a wet lick to the cheek in return. His eyes traced the steamer's bulky lines, then he looked to the far-off horizon.

The nation is taking shape, he thought; and he realized from firsthand experience that the costs were high. It would be a long time before differences would be settled between two conflicting races, if ever. Fire Canoe Finnegan continued to stare at the images of boat and far horizon. It came to him that this steamboat and others like it would play a substantial role in conquering the west. And he, Clint Finnegan, would be part of it.

Dear Reader,

If you enjoyed reading FIRE CANOE FINNEGAN, please help promote the writers of this book by composing and posting a review on Amazon.com.

Charlie Steel can be contacted at **cowboytales@juno.com** or by writing to him at the following address:

Charlie Steel
c/o Condor Publishing, Inc.
PO Box 39
Lincoln, Michigan 48742

Warm greetings from Condor Publishing, Inc.
Gail Heath, publisher

CPSIA information can be obtained
at www.ICGtesting.com
Printed in the USA
BVHW031017310520
580635BV00001B/27

9 781931 079129